Praise

“A gently paced lov … you care what happens to them.”

—***RT Book Reviews*** on *A Place to Call Home*

“A fine portrait of a heroine faced with true-to-life guilt.”

—***RT Book Reviews*** on *A Time to Love*

“Irene Hannon wins our hearts with an uplifting story of love and healing.”

—***RT Book Reviews*** on *Till There Was You*

“Hannon’s multithread plot is woven beautifully together to create a tapestry that will enchant romantics of all ages.”

—***Publishers Weekly*** on *One Perfect Spring*

“Inspiring prose and embraceable characters…capture the reader from the very first pages.”

—***New York Journal of Books*** on *That Certain Summer*

“Touching, compelling, and satisfying.”

—***RT Book Reviews*** on *From This Day Forward*

“A great summer read…relatable characters with real-life problems.”

—***Radiant Lit*** on *Seaside Reunion*

“A warmhearted journey from loss and guilt to self-forgiveness and love.”

—***RT Book Reviews*** on *Once Upon Nantucket*

“A tender and intriguing tale of heartache, loss, and love.”

—***Goodreads*** review on *Crossroads*

“A delightful read...the realism and tenderness draw you into the story.”

—***RT Book Reviews*** on *The Way Home*

“An intense, emotional, thought-provoking read.”

—***Best Reads (2010-2020)*** on *Child of Grace*

A Place to Call Home

CIRCLE OF FRIENDS—BOOK 1
ENCORE EDITION

IRENE HANNON

First edition published 1997 by Harlequin Love Inspired as *Home for the Holidays*
Encore Edition published 2025 by Irene Hannon
(An Encore Edition is a previously published novel that has been revised and reissued with a new cover.)

ISBN 9781970116465

To Tom—
my friend, my hero, my love.

1

It was a good news/bad news scenario—but the bad news outweighed the good.

Nick Sinclair took a slow breath.

Winning the commission to design a new headquarters building for the Midwest Regional Arts Center was huge. It could move his architectural career into the limelight.

But George Thompson's mandate that he consider a no-name landscaping company to design the grounds could sabotage his efforts. No matter how striking his building might be, the setting was critical. First impressions mattered.

Struggling to maintain a placid expression, he crossed an ankle over a knee as he sat across from George's desk. "I'm not familiar with Taylor Landscaping."

"You will be." George rested his elbows on his desk and steepled his fingers. "Great company. Small and relatively new, creative yet practical. Several of the arts center board members have used them. In fact, they did the landscaping at my new house. My wife said they were great to work with. Very professional. And they stayed on budget."

Nick fought back a wave of panic.

This was going from bad to worse.

In general, small residential landscapers weren't equipped to do large commercial jobs. And one weak link was all it took to ruin an otherwise great job.

Or at the very least make his life miserable.

Nick smoothed down his tie, keeping his tone conversational as he responded. "I'm sure they're very competent at what they do, but this job is on a different scale than the grounds of a private home. I've worked with an established firm for several years that I think you'll find—"

"Nick." George held up his hand. "Providing opportunities for young talent is in keeping with the philosophy of the Arts Center. As a matter of fact, it's one of the reasons we chose your firm to design it. I think it's only fair that we give this company a chance, don't you?"

Checkmate.

The Arts Center board *could* have chosen a well-established architectural firm for this project. Instead, the board members—all influential St. Louis business people—were giving him a shot at it.

It was hard to argue that Taylor Landscaping didn't deserve a chance too.

"I see your point." Even if he didn't like the notion of a wet-behind-the-ears firm getting its break at his expense.

"Good. Give them a look, get a bid. I think you'll be impressed. If you're not, we'll talk again."

"Fair enough. I'll contact them and set up a meeting. Why don't we move on to the proposed schedule?"

By the time he left George's office half an hour later, all of the details had been finalized…but his mood hadn't improved.

Stepping outside into the cold, gusty March wind, he scowled at the dark clouds overhead as he strode across the parking lot to his car.

Maybe this Taylor Landscaping could handle the job. But

unless the owner did an amazing sell job on him he intended to take the slim out George had given him and make his case that the firm he'd intended to recommend would do a far better job.

Half an hour later, when he walked through the door of his office, he was no less agitated. After giving the receptionist a distracted nod, he glanced at the two part-time drafting pros at work in a large, airy room, then continued to his partner's office.

The other half of Sinclair and Stevens glanced up from his computer with a hopeful look when he entered. "Well?"

"We got the job, but there's a complication. Have you ever heard of Taylor Landscaping?"

Jack squinted. Shook his head. "I don't think so. Why?"

"The board of the Arts Center *strongly* recommended them for the landscape design."

"Is that bad? What do *you* know about Taylor Landscaping?"

"Nothing. That's the point. It's a newer outfit. I doubt it has much of a track record."

"Sort of like Sinclair and Stevens?" Jack arched an eyebrow.

Nick huffed out a breath. "You sound like George."

"Can't argue with the truth." He folded his arms. Leaned back in his chair. "Why don't you keep cool until you check them out? This firm could be a diamond in the rough."

"It could also be a lump of coal that undermines the commission of my career—and the reputation of Sinclair and Stevens." Nick began to pace. "You know how hard we've worked to get this far. Fourteen-hour days for three long years, in a cramped office with barely room for two desks. We've done okay, but this could move us into the big league. It will make or break our reputation with the movers and shakers in this town."

Jack's brow crimped. "I get how important this job is. But if Taylor Landscaping doesn't cut it, the door's open to other options, right?"

"About half an inch."

"Look, before we jump to conclusions, why don't you check out this company? I trust your judgment. If you're not satisfied with them, tell George. I'll back you up, but this project is your baby, Nick. You went after it, and you did the preliminary design the committee selected. You're the one who has to feel comfortable with the landscaper because you're the one who'll have to work with them."

He sighed. Raked his fingers through his hair. "You're right. Condemning without a trial isn't fair. I'll give the owner a call first thing in the morning."

And hope his worst fears didn't come to pass.

* * *

At nine o'clock the next morning Nick tapped Taylor Landscaping's number into his cell.

The phone rang once. Twice. Three times.

By the sixth ring he was drumming his fingers on the desk.

What kind of outfit was this, anyway? Hadn't anyone ever told them an unanswered phone meant lost business? And why wasn't the call rolling to voicemail if no one was available to pick up?

Just as he was about to disconnect, a slightly breathless female voice answered. "Taylor Landscaping."

Finally.

He straightened up. "This is Nick Sinclair from Sinclair and Stevens. I'd like to speak with Mr. Taylor."

A beat ticked by. "Do you mean the owner?" There was a hint of amusement in the woman's voice.

He frowned.

What was that all about?

"Yes."

"Everyone's out at a job site right now."

Nick swiveled toward the window in his office, where the first hint of purple was visible on the redbud trees. He could leave a message—but it might not be a bad idea to see this outfit at work.

"Why don't you give me the address and I'll swing by? I have business to discuss with the owner."

A beat ticked by.

"I guess that would be okay. Hang on a minute."

Once the woman relayed the address, Nick ended the call. Tapped his pen against the slip of paper.

The job was in a residential area of large homes and expansive grounds.

Not too shabby.

But it wasn't a commercial commission.

He glanced at his watch. If he hurried, he could pay a visit to the owner of Taylor Landscaping before his ten-thirty meeting.

Half an hour later, Nick pulled up to the job site. Four people dressed in jeans and work shirts were at work. Two wrestled with a large boulder. Next to them, a mustached guy fiddled with a jackhammer. Another worker, who appeared to be only a teenager, stood apart with a hose, watering what appeared to be freshly planted azalea bushes.

It was impossible to determine who among the motley crew could be the owner.

Since the kid with the hose was closest, best to start with him. Besides, the guy with the jackhammer had put it to use, and the bone-jarring noise was already giving him a headache.

Nick slid from behind the wheel and scanned the site as he crossed to the guy with the hose, whose back was to him.

The house was new, built on a vacant lot in an established neighborhood. The ground had been cleared during construction, and a complete landscaping job was under way. The work appeared to be in the early stages, and it was difficult to tell whether a cohesive plan had been developed. But a well-maintained pickup truck bearing the name Taylor Landscaping was parked in the circular driveway, and the crew seemed energetic.

All at once the jackhammer stopped, and in the blessed silence Nick hurried toward the guy with the hose. Tapped him on the shoulder.

The young man jerked. Swung around. Drenched him in the most embarrassing possible place.

As the cold water hit his skin, Nick gave a startled exclamation. Then he lunged for the hose and yanked it in a different direction. "Watch what you're doing!"

"I'm…I'm really sorry."

As the teenager stammered an apology, Nick pulled out his handkerchief and tried without success to sop up the moisture. "That solves everything, doesn't it? When I leave here, I'm going to an important meeting. How am I supposed to explain this?" He waved a hand over the front of his slacks. It was doubtful the fabric would be dry by then.

"You could say you had an accident."

At the mildly amused voice, Nick glanced up. The worker who'd offered that wisecrack wore a baseball cap and dark sunglasses.

"Very funny." He glared at the smart aleck. "Which one of you is Mr. Taylor?" He waved a hand over the crew.

"Who?"

He gritted his teeth. "The owner."

After a moment, the worker flipped off the baseball cap, releasing a cascade of strawberry blond hair caught back in a ponytail. Then she removed the glasses to reveal two startlingly green eyes. "You're looking at her." Her husky voice now sounded even more amused.

As Nick processed that news, he stifled a groan.

This was not beginning well.

Even if more than eighty percent of landscaping businesses were headed by men in the male-dominated industry, assuming the owner was a man was exceedingly bad form in this day and age.

"Laura, I—I'm really sorry."

She turned her attention to the young man holding the hose, who looked stricken. "It's okay, Jimmy. No permanent damage was done." She smiled. Reached over and gave his arm a reassuring squeeze. "The azaleas at the end could use more water. Why don't you finish up over there?" Then she called over her shoulder to the other two men. "I'll be with you guys in a few minutes. Do what you can in the meantime."

After taking a deep breath, she refocused on him, the warmth in her eyes and her tone chilling. "What can I do for you?"

Oh, boy.

He might not be thrilled about the idea of Taylor Landscaping working on the arts center, but inciting the ire of the owner hadn't been on his agenda.

The question now was how to make amends.

Before he could formulate an approach, her eyes narrowed and she propped her hands on her hips. "Look, mister, I don't have all day. I've got a lot of work to do."

Backbreaking work, from what he'd seen. She might be in the five-seven range, using his six-one height as a gauge, but her lithe, willowy figure didn't look suited to hard physical labor.

"Why isn't he doing the heavy lifting?" He motioned toward the young man with the hose.

"He's only sixteen. That would be too much for him."

"And it's not for you?"

"I'm used to this kind of work. He isn't."

"How can you run this company if you're out in the field doing manual labor?"

Her chin lifted. "Not that it's any of your business, but we happen to be one person short today."

"As a matter of fact, it does happen to be my business."

Twin creases dented her brow. "I'm not following you."

"I'm Nick Sinclair, of Sinclair and Stevens. We're designing the new Regional Arts Center, and George Thompson suggested we consider your firm for the landscape portion."

Shock flattened her features. Then she bit her lip as a flush crept across her cheeks.

If he'd discombobulated her, fine. Let her sweat it out. He certainly was. From what he'd seen so far, Taylor Landscaping wasn't ready for prime time.

Still, as the silence lengthened and the spunky animation in her vivid green eyes was replaced by distress, guilt nipped at his conscience.

After all, he was the one who'd appeared on the scene uninvited and disrupted what otherwise seemed to be a relatively smooth operation. Then he'd overreacted to a simple mistake.

He'd also made a huge faux pas by assuming the owner was a man.

Maybe an apology was in order.

But the woman across from him spoke first. "Do you think we could start over?"

"I'm game."

She wiped her hand on her jeans and held it out. "Laura Taylor."

Nick grasped her fingers and returned her firm grip. "Nice to meet you."

The twist of her lips suggested she wasn't buying his pleasantry. "I'm sorry about that." She waved toward the embarrassing water spot. "Jimmy spooks easily."

"Isn't sixteen a little young to be working on a crew like this?"

"Yes, but he needed a job. I hired him through Christian Youth Outreach. Have you heard of it?"

"No."

She sighed. "Unfortunately, too few people have. It's an organization that provides support for young people from troubled homes. Jimmy is part of a work-study program sponsored by the group. He works for me part-time, to earn money for college." She glanced toward him. "He'll need all the help he can get. I'm just doing my bit."

As Laura Taylor watched the young man, Nick took a closer look at her.

She was older than he'd first thought. Early thirties, in all likelihood. A fan of barely perceptible lines radiated from the corners of her eyes, and faint shadows hung under her lower lashes. The slight, permanent creases in her brow suggested she was serious by nature or under stress—or perhaps both.

And she was obviously a hard worker. She ran a company, which was no small feat, and also worked on job sites when necessary. Yet she still found time to help others.

Admirable.

But it didn't alleviate his concerns about Taylor Landscaping's ability to handle the Regional Arts Center project. Hard work was important, but talent and creativity were the critical components. How her company would fare on that score remained to be seen. And until he had a handle on that, he wasn't about to make any promises.

"Why don't we defer our discussion about the arts center?" He glanced at his watch. "You're busy, and I have a meeting to attend. Could we get together tomorrow at one?"

"That would be fine."

He withdrew a business card from his pocket and handed it to her. "Sorry for the interruption today."

"No worries." She took the card, then tugged her baseball cap back on and settled her sunglasses on her nose. "I'll see you tomorrow."

As she strode back to join her crew, the jarring reverberations of the jackhammer started up again.

Nick walked back to his car, the headache he'd had earlier returning with a vengeance.

How this would all play out after their meeting tomorrow was unknown—but one thing was certain.

The potential partnership of Taylor Landscaping and Sinclair and Stevens was off to a rocky start.

2

He was twenty minutes late for his meeting with Laura Taylor.

And since her truck was in his office's small parking lot, she was waiting for him.

Nick swung into a spot and set the brake.

Yesterday hadn't gone well, and his tardiness wasn't going to help smooth the waters.

But all he could do at this point was apologize.

He slid out of the car, strode into the lobby, and paused at their administrative assistant's desk. "I assume Laura Taylor is here."

"Yes. When you weren't back at one, Jack came out and got her. I think they're in his office."

"Thanks, Connie. Anything urgent I need to deal with?"

"No. You're good."

Not really, but he let that pass.

As he detoured to his desk to deposit his briefcase, the sound of voices from Jack's office drifted down the hall. It was impossible to make out the conversation, but his partner's sudden laugh suggested he and Laura Taylor had hit it off.

Good.

Maybe if Jack had kept her entertained, she'd be less upset about the late start for their meeting.

After shrugging out of his jacket, he rolled up the sleeves of his dress shirt, loosened his tie, and flexed the muscles in his shoulders. A few minutes to chill out in the wake of his marathon lunch meeting with a difficult client would have been welcome, but he'd kept the owner of Taylor Landscaping waiting long enough.

As he approached Jack's office, the animated conversation grew louder. His partner was half visible through the open door, hip propped on desk, ankles crossed, arms folded. But Nick gave him no more than a passing glance, directing his attention instead to Laura Taylor.

She was sitting in one of the chairs by the desk, angled slightly away from him, legs crossed, while she chatted with Jack.

Giving her a slow perusal, Nick slowed his pace.

Her attire was the same as yesterday—jeans, a cotton work shirt, and sturdy boots. The baseball cap was missing, but her hair was once again caught back in a ponytail that emphasized the fine bone structure of her face. Her shirt was tucked in, a hemp belt encircled a waist that seemed no more than a handspan in circumference, and worn jeans outlined her long legs.

Funny.

Despite her workmanlike attire, Laura Taylor radiated more femininity than most of the professional women he knew, who sported salon manicures and wore designer clothes.

His gaze moved on to her hands, which were resting on the arms of her chair. She had long, graceful fingers, but it was clear that manicures weren't part of her life. Her nails were cut short and left unpolished, and her hands looked somewhat work-worn.

Thanks to struggles with boulders like the one yesterday, no doubt.

Which bothered him on a number of levels, for some strange reason. As did the shadows he'd noticed under her lashes during their first meet-up.

Before he could dwell on his odd reaction, she shifted toward him, and a flicker of anxiety sparked to life in her eyes as their gazes met.

As if sensing the change in mood, Jack angled toward the door. "Come on in, Nick. Laura and I were just getting acquainted."

Nick continued forward as he spoke to her. "I'm sorry about the delay. My lunch meeting took longer than I expected. I hope the wait didn't inconvenience you."

"No. I've enjoyed chatting with Jack. I'm just going back to the job site when I finish here."

"Still one person short?"

"Yes."

"In that case, let's try to make this as brief as possible." He shifted his attention to his partner. "Do you want to sit in?"

"I'd like to, but I have a two o'clock I need to prepare for."

"Then we'll let you get to it. Ms. Taylor, why don't we meet in the conference room? There's more space to spread out the plans."

"It's Mrs." She picked up her portfolio from beside her chair and stood as he discreetly checked out her left hand. Yep, there was a ring. "I'm ready whenever you are. Jack, it was nice meeting you."

"My pleasure."

As Nick stepped aside to let her precede him out the door, Jack grinned and gave him a thumbs-up.

Nice that he and Laura had clicked, but he was more interested in her abilities as a landscaper than her social graces or charisma.

He followed her down the hall, trying to ignore the faint, pleasing fragrance that emanated from her hair. "Next door on the right. Go in and make yourself comfortable while I get the elevations."

She nodded and disappeared inside.

After making a U-turn, he returned to his office. Paused to lean on his desk, palms flat, and take a deep, steadying breath as he tried to figure out why Laura Taylor unsettled him.

Maybe it was the juxtaposition of strength and vulnerability that radiated from her. As a small-business owner, she had to be independent, tough, smart, and ambitious to survive. Yet unlike many of the professional women of his acquaintance, there was an innate gentleness about her that hinted at a tender, caring heart.

It was an intriguing—and appealing—combination.

But it had nothing to do with the matter at hand.

With an impatient huff, he straightened up and circled his desk to retrieve the elevations.

From here on out, he was going to focus on Laura Taylor's professional qualifications.

Period.

He retraced his steps down the hall, and when he entered the conference room he found her still standing. "Sorry to keep you waiting." He set the printouts on the table. "Have a seat."

She chose a chair, unzipped her portfolio, and extracted a pile of printed material while he settled in next to her. A hum of tension thrummed through the air as she folded her hands on the table and looked at him. "Before we talk about the arts center job, I have a few things to say."

"Okay." He leaned back in his seat.

"If you're like most architects, I expect you have

established relationships with a group of proven, reliable contractors. And I assume that for a prestigious job like the Regional Arts Center you'd prefer to use one of them."

The lady was direct.

"We do have a preferred list of landscaping firms."

"And we're not on it. Meaning we're a wild card for you." Her tone was businesslike and matter-of-fact. "I appreciate the board's confidence in us, but for a collaboration between us to be most productive you have to be comfortable. So I brought photos of our work, some blueprints of my designs, a list of all our jobs since the business began six years ago, a summary of my academic and professional credentials, and client references."

Impressive.

"I appreciate your thoroughness."

She lifted one shoulder. "I understand why you'd be concerned about using us, since we've never done a project on the scale of the Regional Arts Center. But I know we can do an exceptional job."

As he studied her earnest eyes, taut posture, and tightly clenched fingers, an image of her struggling with the boulder yesterday flashed through his mind.

It was clear she was a hands-on, hard worker, and that this project meant as much to her as it did to him—maybe more.

He called up a smile. "For the record, I'm keeping an open mind. Why don't we look at some of the photos first?"

There was an almost imperceptible softening in the rigid line of her shoulders.

They worked their way through all of the material she'd brought, and while it was impressive for what it was, there was nothing remotely on the scale of the Arts Center.

Major red flag, but not unexpected.

When they finished, he once again leaned back in his chair, choosing his words with care. "Your work appears to be excellent, but your firm is small and your focus is clearly residential work. Do you think you're equipped to handle the Arts Center?"

"Yes." No hesitation. "I'll have to add to our crew, but I've been wanting to do that anyway. I was just waiting for the right commission to come along to justify staffing up. As for my ability to do the design, all I'm asking for is a chance to give you my ideas. I won't even charge for spec time."

"No one expects you to work for free."

Her gaze locked with his. "I'll put in however many hours it takes to convince you we can handle this project."

She wanted this job. Bad.

And what did he have to lose by seeing what she could do?

"Why don't you take a look at the elevations first?" He pulled them in front of them. "I can fill you in on the terrain."

"That's not necessary. I've already been to the site."

He arched his eyebrows. "When?"

"This morning. I knew where it was from articles in the paper, so I went over there early and walked around a bit. But I had no idea what your design looked like, or even what direction the building will face, so I can't talk intelligently about landscaping until I see these." She tapped the elevations.

Her initiative was notable.

He unrolled the elevations, and for the next forty-five minutes she pored over them, asking astute questions and taking extensive notes.

When they finished, she set her pen down. "It's a spectacular building. I like the use of natural materials and the seamless integration of contemporary and classical features. It will lend itself beautifully to landscaping that features native plants and trees."

"Any preliminary thoughts on that score?"

Her eyes began to sparkle as she leaned forward to examine the front elevation again. "The entrance could be stunning in the spring with dogwoods and azaleas and redbud trees here and here and here." She pointed as she talked. "And the area around the reflecting pool you've roughed in would be a perfect area for a display of seasonal flowers."

"Sounds interesting."

"I hope you'll give me the opportunity to put some rough designs on paper and meet with you again before you commit to George on a landscaper."

The tension was back in her features as she waited for his verdict, the fingers of her left hand balled into a tight fist on the table.

An illogical urge to reach over and smooth away the smudges under her lower lashes with his thumb swept over him, but he stifled it at once.

Clearing his throat, he gathered up the elevations. "I'm on board with that. Would you like a paper or AutoCAD copy of these elevations?"

She let out a shaky breath. One she'd been holding, perhaps. "AutoCAD would be great. You can email them to me." She dug out a card and handed it over.

"When would you like to get together again?"

"Would a week from today work?"

He gave her a doubtful look. "That's not very long."

"It's enough to do a rough design."

"All right. Should we try one o'clock again?"

"That works." She gathered up her materials, slid them back

into her portfolio, and rose. "Thank you for this opportunity, Mr. Sinclair."

"Why don't we switch to first names?"

"Fine by me."

"I'll walk you out."

He shook her hand when they reached the lobby, lingering to watch through the window as she strode toward her car.

Only when he caught Connie smirking at him did he pivot and start back to his office. "She seems to be quite talented." He kept his tone casual.

"Not hard on the eyes, either."

"She's married."

"Bummer."

"I'm not in the market anyway."

"You and Lauren still an item, or are you back to playing the field?"

"I still see Lauren—when we can make our schedules work."

Connie wrinkled her nose. "How unromantic."

Yeah, it was.

But as with all the women he dated, work had always taken precedence. Dates were penciled in, and it was understood that if a business conflict arose, the personal commitment would be sacrificed. Which was happening more and more…and starting to bother him.

Because he was beginning to want what Jack had—a solid marriage and a family.

As he wandered back down the hall, that vague yearning resurfaced with surprising strength.

And it wasn't hard to pinpoint the reason.

A green-eyed landscaper with amazing strawberry blond

hair who'd somehow managed to awaken a desire for the romance Connie thought was so lacking in his life.

* * *

Three nights later, the ring of her cell phone penetrated Laura's awareness.

She tore her gaze from the monitor on the workstation in a corner of her living room and flicked her phone an annoyed glance. Scanned her watch.

It was after seven, so it had to be a social call. And she had no time for socializing. Not with the commission of a lifetime dangling in front of her.

She refocused on her in-progress arts center landscape design.

When her phone trilled again fifteen minutes later, she paid no attention to it.

But it was harder to ignore the ringing of her doorbell an hour later.

Huffing out a breath, she rubbed her eyes.

She'd promised Nick Sinclair designs in a week with full knowledge that the commitment would appreciably lengthen her already long workdays. But they were going to be even longer if she had too many interruptions.

The bell rang again. And again. And again.

Enough already.

Massaging her neck muscles with one hand, Laura rose and marched over to the door. Peeked through the peephole at the woman on the other side, who was toting a white bag. Blinked.

What on earth was Sam doing here?

She flipped the locks and opened the door for her best

friend. "This is a surprise. Come in."

Sam sauntered in, her pencil skirt and fashionable blazer looking as perfect as they'd no doubt looked when she started her workday hours ago. "Is the battery in your cell dead?"

"What?" Laura frowned as she shut and bolted the door.

"I keep calling and it keeps ringing. And you're obviously here."

"Oh." Warmth crept across her cheeks. "Sorry. I'm on a deadline for what could be the commission that will put Taylor Landscaping on the map, and I don't have time for anything else until next week."

"Including food?"

Sam would ask that.

"I've been eating." Here and there.

"What did you have for dinner?"

"Um…I haven't had dinner yet."

Sam made a show of checking her watch. "May I ask what time you're planning to dine?"

"When I get hungry."

"If you're not hungry at this hour, you must have had a big lunch."

"No." And the apple and yogurt she'd eaten hours ago were long gone. No wonder the enticing smells emanating from the white sack Sam held produced a rumble in her stomach. "Sorry." She pressed her hand against her abdomen.

"You wouldn't want to share some Chinese with me, would you?" Sam waved the bag under her nose.

"I could be persuaded. Why are *you* eating so late?"

"I was showing a house and my clients had to poke into every single nook and cranny." She shook her head, setting her sleek, shoulder-length red hair in motion.

"Bad news for you, good news for me since you brought food. Let's eat."

Sam walked over to the small café table and opened the cartons while Laura set out plates and utensils. "I brought Mongolian beef and cashew chicken. Which do you want?

"Some of both."

"You got it." She began doling out the food.

"You know, I've never understood this mothering complex you have." Laura filled glasses with water. "Not that I'm complaining. But I really can take care of myself."

"Right." Sam sat and took a serving of rice. "I guess that's why you skip meals and work long hours."

"Getting a business off the ground isn't easy. And right now I don't care if I have to stay up every night until two in the morning. If we get this job, it will be worth it."

Sam stared at her. "Is that when you've been going to bed? You can't keep up that kind of pace."

"It's not forever."

"What makes this job so special?"

A pang of guilt shot through her. If she'd had one spare minute she'd already have told Sam her news. "You've heard about the new Regional Arts Center that's going to be built, right?"

"Sure. It's been all over local media."

"I may get a shot at doing the landscaping."

Sam stopped eating, fork poised halfway to her mouth. "Wow. That's big-league stuff. Tell me everything."

While she chowed down, Laura filled her in, concluding with Nick Sinclair's visit to her job site four days ago. "Although I haven't yet figured out how he knew where I was."

"I think I can enlighten you on that."

Laura squinted at her. "What do you know that I don't?"

"I stopped by your office that morning to use the bathroom before I met my next client. I know the key you gave me is supposed to be for emergencies, but believe me, this qualified. Anyway, the phone kept ringing so I answered it. Nick Sinclair was on the line. He asked for *Mr.* Taylor and didn't seem to appreciate my amusement. Your job schedule was on the desk, and I didn't think it would hurt to give him the address. I meant to tell you, but it's been crazy this week."

"I know all about crazy weeks." Laura took another serving of the beef.

"He sounded a bit peeved on the phone, but he did have an intriguing voice. What does he look like?"

Laura called up an image of him. "About six feet tall, dark hair, brown eyes, midthirtyish, sharp dresser." No need to mention his broad shoulders or toned physique that suggested he followed a regular exercise regimen. "To tell you the truth, I've been so intimidated the two times we've met it's everything I can do to speak coherently let alone take inventory."

"Do me a favor, kiddo. Next time, take inventory."

"Why?"

Sam rolled her eyes. "Do you have to ask?"

No.

And this was not a subject she wanted to discuss.

"For all I know, he's married. Besides, we've been over this before."

"True, but I haven't changed my mind. It's been almost ten years, Laura. You could do with some male companionship."

"Correction. I can do *without* it." She stabbed a piece of broccoli.

Sam gave a dramatic sigh. "I wish you'd make an effort. Is this guy nice?"

"He wasn't the first time we met. He was chauvinistic and rude."

"Well, he *had* just been doused with a hose." Sam scooped up a forkful of rice. "What about the second time you met?"

Laura chased the last piece of chicken around her plate.

That had been a different story.

Yes, he'd been late, but he'd not only apologized, he'd spent a chunk of his day looking at all the material she'd brought and walking her through the elevations for the arts center. He'd also agreed to let her submit preliminary design ideas before locking in a landscaper.

Despite his more mellow attitude, however—and much as she wanted this job—the thought of working with him was unsettling. And it sent some very unwanted tingles racing along her nerve endings.

"He was nicer." She captured the chicken. Put it in her mouth. Chewed. "But he…he kind of makes me nervous."

Sam's expression brightened. "That's a start."

Shaking her head, Laura set her fork down and reached for a fortune cookie. "You're a hopeless romantic."

"Correction. I'm a *hopeful* romantic." She took a cookie too. Broke it open. "What does your fortune say?"

Laura read it. Crumpled it in her fingers as warmth crept across her cheeks. "These things are stupid."

"I think they're fun. What does it say?" Sam cocked her head, interest glinting in her eyes.

"If I tell you, will you promise not to make any comments?"

"Sure."

Laura smoothed out the fortune. "It says, 'His heart was yours from the moment you met.'"

Sam didn't say a word.

She just smiled.

3

The late-afternoon air was muggy, the string quartet at the arts center groundbreaking party could barely be heard above the clamor of the crowd that had been driven under the large tent by a sudden June shower, and his champagne glass was empty.

Grimacing, Nick adjusted his bow tie as he tucked himself into an empty corner. He'd schmoozed with all the right people, smiled for the photographers, and participated in the ribbon-cutting ceremony. Now all he wanted to do was go home, shed his tux, and relax.

Funny.

Despite the festive surroundings and the enthusiastic praise his design had received in the press and from the board, his spirits felt as flat as the residue of champagne in his glass.

Go figure.

He gave the crowd another sweep. Froze as he suddenly realized why he kept searching the clusters of guests.

He was looking for Laura. Had been since he'd arrived. Because the party didn't feel complete without her.

Huh.

He twirled the stem of the champagne flute.

Yes, he'd enjoyed her company during their meetings these past two months, since he'd given the green light for her involvement. But since when had he begun to look forward so much to seeing her? To eliciting a rare smile from this woman who was far too serious, seemed to work way too hard, and whose vocabulary didn't appear to include the words fun or leisure? From what he'd gathered over the past few weeks, she had zero downtime.

Heck, for all he knew she'd had to forego today's party because she'd been called to a job site.

He curbed a sudden surge of annoyance.

Where was her husband in all this? Didn't he care how hard she worked? Or perhaps he was ill or unemployed, and Laura had to carry the burden of support for—

"Nick! I've been trying to track you down for an hour." George Thompson spoke behind him, and he angled toward the man. "I wanted to congratulate you again on an outstanding job. I've heard nothing but compliments from everyone who's looked at the scale model."

He called up a smile. "Thank you. Great party, by the way."

"Except for the weather. But the rain's letting up. Let's hope the crowd moves outside. This tent is a steam bath. Well, enjoy yourself."

As the man moved off, guests did begin to make their way out of the tent.

Hallelujah.

Nick scanned the thinning crowd again. Maybe he could spot a server with a fresh tray of something other than champagne. A little bit of the fizzy beverage went a long way.

Halfway through his perusal, a woman seated in the far corner of the tent caught his eye. She was angled sideways, her body blocked from his view by a tuxedoed figure, but the killer legs revealed under a fashionably short black skirt would make any man do a double take.

Suddenly she uncrossed those legs and stood. She now stood totally hidden from his view by the man in the tuxedo.

So much for that brief pleasant interlude.

Just as he started to turn away to go in search of a soft drink, the woman attempted to move out from behind the man.

But he gripped her arm and backed her farther into the corner.

Nick hesitated.

Most women were more than capable of taking care of themselves in situations like that. Heck, the man could be her husband—or an important guest it wouldn't be wise to offend.

But when the woman moved to one side in another attempt to extricate herself, his heart stuttered.

It was Laura.

And now it was clear why he hadn't spotted her earlier. Her black cocktail dress with skinny straps held in place by rhinestone clips was night and day from her usual jeans. And her standard ponytail was gone. Today, her hair was loose and full, falling in soft, shimmering waves past her creamy shoulders. The eye makeup and lipstick were also new.

She looked chic and sophisticated and polished, and she seemed as comfortable here as she did on a construction site.

Wow.

Before he could get his eyes back in their sockets, she made yet another futile attempt to detach herself from the man's grasp.

Nick surged forward, maneuvering his way through the crowd as he kept her in his sights. It was obvious she was trying her best to be polite and not make a scene, but as he drew close and the fear in her eyes registered, his gut clenched.

Picking up his pace, he grabbed two champagne flutes from the tray of a passing waiter and took a calming breath as he drew close to her. "I've been looking everywhere for you, Laura. I finally found the champagne." He managed to keep his tone even despite the anger coursing through him.

Her gaze flew to his, and the relief in her eyes was almost palpable. "Thanks. I wondered where you went." Her voice sounded a bit unsteady, but she followed his lead and took the glass he held out.

Her fingers were icy when they brushed his.

The fortyish, balding man looked from him to Laura, his flushed face suggesting he was overheated or had downed more than his share of champagne. "You two are together? Sorry. Why didn't you say so?" He removed his hand from Laura's arm, leaving a red mark on her skin. "I think I'll get another drink."

As he disappeared into the crowd, Laura set her glass on the table next to her and took a deep breath. "You have perfect timing." The corners of her lips rose, but her smile was strained and a quiver ran through her voice.

"Not always." He nodded toward the glass of champagne she'd set down. "Maybe you should drink that."

She wrinkled her nose. "No, thanks. Enough alcohol has been consumed on these premises already."

"I won't argue with that."

"I don't have anything against moderate drinking, but I have no tolerance for people who overindulge." She pulled a mirror from a purse on the table and adjusted an earring. Buying herself a moment to regain her composure, perhaps.

Nick took a slow sip of champagne he didn't want, giving her the time she needed. "I don't, either. Let's hope your admirer isn't planning to drive home."

"I know." She set the silver, filigreed mirror on the edge of the table. Wrapped her arms around her middle. "Thank you for your help. I'm not…I don't handle those kinds of situations very well."

"You shouldn't have to. No woman should."

At his quiet comment, her lips twisted. "That sounds good in theory anyway." She exhaled. "I think I'll head home."

"Did you work all day?"

"Most of the day. I was on a job site until about three hours ago."

He arched an eyebrow as he gave her a quick head-to-toe. "That's quite a transformation."

One side of her mouth quirked up. "As my best friend says, I clean up well."

"Better than well."

The husky comment was out before he could stop it, but he was saved from having to mitigate that personal comment when a passing partygoer tripped over a chair and crashed into them, jarring the table and throwing Laura off balance.

"Sorry." The man mumbled his apology as Nick grabbed her arm to steady her.

The guy drifted off, weaving slightly, and she shook her head. Reached for her purse. "I'm definitely done for the day." The quiver was back in her voice. "All I want to do is go home and chill."

"Would you like me to walk you to your car?" Because apparently her husband wasn't here.

"No, thanks. But I appreciate the offer. Good night."

He watched her thread through the thinning crowd, jamming a hand into the pocket of his slacks as she disappeared.

Strange that she'd seemed so shaken by her encounter with the tipsy guests. Certainly the situation had been unpleasant, but there'd been no real danger. Yet the fear in her eyes had been acute. It was the kind only a protective, caring hug would banish.

But he'd done all he could for her. Her husband would have to take care of any physical consoling. He ought to put the incident out of his mind and call it a night.

As he turned to set his glass on the table, a glint of silver caught his eye.

Laura's filigreed mirror rested on the grass at his feet.

It must have fallen when the other guest careened into them, jarring the table.

He picked it up and examined it. The old-fashioned mirror looked like an antique. A family heirloom, perhaps?

Weighing it in his hand, he peered after her. If he hurried, maybe he could catch her before—

"Nick, do you have a minute?"

He shifted around. One of the arts center board members was walking toward him.

Pocketing the mirror, he called up a smile and spent the next few minutes listening to the man discourse on the importance of art to the St. Louis community and how the new center would bring more attention to the cultural riches of the city.

When the man at last wound down, Nick strode out of the tent and to the parking area, which was considerably less crowded than it had been earlier. But Laura's truck was nowhere to be seen.

She was gone.

Better call and let her know he'd found the mirror in case it was a treasured keepsake. If she realized it was missing, she could panic—and she'd had enough stress for one night.

He started to pull out his phone. Hesitated as an idea began to percolate in his mind.

Why not drop it off at her place before he headed home? It

shouldn't be difficult to find her address. He might even have a chance to meet the elusive Mr. Taylor.

And maybe get a handle on why Laura never mentioned the man she'd married .

* * *

Laura stirred the spaghetti sauce, sampled a taste, and smiled.

Perfection.

But then, Gram's recipe never failed. It was one of those things you could always count on.

And there weren't a lot of those in this world.

Her mouth flattened.

She could always count on her family, of course. And Sam.

But not men. Or at least not her judgment of them.

She gave the sauce another stir, set the spoon down, and sighed.

Getting melancholy because of an incident she'd blown out of all proportion was dumb. So what if the guy at the ground-breaking party had stirred up old hurts? She wasn't the only one in the world with painful memories, and it was time she laid hers to rest.

And she'd made progress on that score. Three or four years ago she would have been a basket case after today's scene.

Although it was possible she *would* have freaked out if Nick hadn't come along. She'd been on the verge.

She took off her apron, tossed it over the back of a kitchen chair, and wandered down the hall as a fanciful image of a knight charging in to slay a dragon flashed through her mind.

Shaking her head, she entered the bedroom and reached around to unzip her dress. She was far too old for fairy tales.

And thinking about Nick in those terms was beyond foolish. Even if she was in the market for romance, fixating on a business colleague was bad form.

After stepping out of her dress, Laura made her way toward the closet, pausing as she caught sight of her reflection in the dresser mirror.

She was still too thin. Or, to use Joe's term, bony. Which translated to unappealing and undesirable and ugly.

A familiar knot formed in her stomach, and she fisted her hands.

You'd think, after more than a decade, she'd stop being self-conscious about her body. After all, she'd gained a little weight over the years.

But not enough to give her the womanly curves men seemed to appreciate.

Except for the drunk at today's party.

She suppressed a shudder and moved past the mirror.

That kind of attention she could do without.

Which was one of the reasons she hid behind androgynous work clothes. Besides being practical, that attire was safer. As was the solitary life she'd created for herself off the job, where no one made demands of her, belittled her, or hurt her. It was a secure, if insulated, existence.

And she'd been perfectly fine with that life, despite Sam's prodding to give romance another go—until Nick had entered her orbit and awakened hormones best left undisturbed.

Which was bad news.

She continued to the chest of drawers. Pulled out a pair of shorts and a T-shirt.

There was a simple explanation for her reaction to him, of course. She'd spent more time in his presence these past few weeks than she'd spent with any man in years. And he'd turned out to be charming and warm and personable, despite their rocky start. Any woman would find him attractive and appealing.

But no matter what Sam thought, she'd never again let a man into her heart.

It was too risky.

And since her self-imposed exile from the dating scene had protected her well for ten years, why fix what wasn't broken?

Even if a few cracks had suddenly appeared in her armor.

* * *

This could be a mistake.

Nick eased back on the gas pedal as he turned onto Laura's street.

It was possible her husband wouldn't appreciate him dropping by, even to return a lost item. And the last thing he wanted to do was cause her any further distress.

"You have arrived at your destination."

As his phone spoke, he coasted to a stop in front of a four-family brick flat on the city's south side and gave the area a sweep.

Definitely not the best part of town.

In fact, it bordered on seedy.

He frowned.

Money must be tighter than he'd thought. Not sufficient to provide her with an income that would pay the rent on a West County condo with tennis courts and a swimming pool and health club, like the one he lived in.

Sometimes life wasn't fair.

Laura appeared to work just as hard—if not harder—than

he did, with much less to show for it. Even in his leaner years, his lifestyle had never been this bare-bones.

It was also possible she'd prefer that business acquaintances not know about her modest, no-frills living quarters.

He was here now, though. May as well return the mirror. If she or her husband were unhappy about his appearance, he'd beat a hasty retreat.

A few teenagers on a neighboring porch gave him a once-over when he slid from behind the wheel. Or maybe they were eyeing his sports car.

He hesitated.

Was it safe to leave it here?

But he wasn't staying long. It would be fine for a few minutes.

He hoped.

After locking the car, he strode inside the building, took the steps to the second floor two at a time, and rang the bell beside a door with a peephole.

After thirty seconds, he tried again.

Half a minute later, the knob rattled and Laura pulled the door open, brow puckered. "This is a surprise."

And not the most welcome one, based on her wary tone.

But it was hard to formulate a response as he tried not to stare at the shorts that hugged her hips and revealed even more of her amazing legs than the cocktail dress had. Or the T-shirt that hinted at soft, appealing curves and was a perfect match for her blue eyes.

He stifled the urge to reach up and loosen his bow tie, which suddenly felt too tight.

"Nick?"

At her prompt, he cleared his throat and tried to will the

surge of heat on his neck to recede. "I, uh, found this on the ground after you left the party." He fished the mirror out of his pocket and held it out. "I thought you might be worried when you realized it was missing. It looks like it might be valuable."

Eyes widening, she let out a soft gasp and reached for it, cradling it in her hands. "I have no idea about its monetary worth, but its sentimental value is priceless. My grandfather gave this to my grandmother on their wedding day. It was one of her most treasured possessions."

"Then I'm glad it's safe and sound."

She squinted at him. "Did you drive all the way over here to return this? You could have just called."

Yeah, he could have.

He shrugged. "I didn't have anything else on my agenda for the evening." An aroma that hinted of garlic and spices wafted past his nose, activating his salivary glands. She must be in the middle of making dinner. "Well…" He took a step back. "I don't want to interrupt your evening. It smells like you're cooking."

"Yes. Spaghetti sauce. It's an old family recipe."

He hitched up one side of his mouth. "You were smart to plan on dinner after the party. Those bite-sized hors d'oeuvres were tasty but not very filling."

"They *were* kind of small." Her frown returned. "You must be hungry. And your good deed delayed your dinner."

"I won't starve." He pulled out his keys.

She bit her lower lip. "Look, would you, uh, like to stay for spaghetti? I appreciate you making a special trip to return the mirror, and a simple thank you doesn't seem sufficient."

She was inviting him to dinner?

His spirits ticked up.

But how would her husband feel about an unexpected guest?

"The offer is tempting." He called up a smile. "Are you certain your husband won't mind?"

A shaft of pain flared in her eyes, but a nanosecond later her features went flat. "My husband is dead."

Despite her matter-of-fact tone, a shock wave rippled through him. "I'm sorry. When we met you said you preferred the title Mrs., so I assumed you were still married."

"The title and the ring make my life simpler. Most guys back off if they think you're married, and the ones who don't aren't worth getting to know anyway."

In other words, she wasn't interested in dating.

Was she a new widow, perhaps?

He shifted his weight from one foot to the other. If he probed too much, she could shut down. But maybe a question or two would be okay. "If I may ask, is your loss recent?"

"No. He died ten years ago." She took a deep breath. "So would you like to share my spaghetti?"

No more questions would be answered—but there was also no more doubt in his mind about whether to stay. Because now he was more intrigued by her than ever.

"Yes."

She stepped back, and as he crossed into a tiny foyer she shut the door and slid the bolt into place. "Make yourself comfortable." She waved toward the living room.

Nick gave it a fast perusal.

Interior design wasn't his forte, but the room had an English country feel. Floral-patterned chintz covered the couches and chairs, and an old trunk topped by a bouquet of flowers served as a coffee table. The warm, homey feeling was enhanced by soft yellow walls and filmy curtains. Only the desk with a laptop and large monitor, tucked into one corner beside a counter that separated the living room from the galley kitchen, seemed out of place.

"Very nice."

"Thanks. It's amazing what a little paint, a needle and thread, and elbow grease can do. Go ahead and take a seat while I get dinner on the table."

"Why don't I help?"

"Um..." She wiped her palms down her shorts. "The kitchen is kind of small, and there's not a lot to do."

He called up his most engaging grin. "I'm not a bad salad maker. If you were planning to have one, I could do that while you finish the spaghetti."

"That wasn't on my menu—but I do have salad fixings."

"Salad goes great with Italian food. Why don't you let me tackle that?"

"I guess that would be okay."

While he shrugged out of his jacket, removed his cuff links, and rolled up his sleeves, she sidled behind a wingback chair, waves of tension rolling off her as she watched him.

His fingers froze as he started to untie his bow tie.

She was uber stressed.

And much as he'd like to stay, if his presence was causing her distress he ought to leave.

"Is something wrong?" He kept his voice conversational.

"No." But her tight grip on the back of the chair in front of her said otherwise.

"You seem a little tense." A gross understatement.

She tucked a long lock of hair behind her ear. "It's been a long day. And I'm, uh, not used to having a dinner guest."

"Would you like me to leave?"

"No." She let out a slow breath. "To tell you the truth, it will be kind of nice to have someone to talk to while I eat. I'll meet you in the kitchen."

With that, she pivoted, circled the counter that separated the two rooms, and crossed to the stove, keeping her back to him.

Slowly Nick loosened his tie—but rather than remove it, he let the two ends dangle.

Why was Laura so skittish? Was it him…or was she like this around all men?

Could be the latter, if she'd had a few too many encounters like the one with the tipsy partygoer this afternoon.

But she had nothing to fear from him. On the contrary.

And he'd prove that to her if she gave him half a chance.

Starting tonight.

4

Pulse skittering, Laura stirred the spaghetti sauce as a wave of second thoughts crashed over her.

Inviting Nick to dinner had been the polite thing to do, but now that he'd joined her in the tiny kitchen, his intimidating presence seemed to fill the cramped space.

Not that she was afraid of him in a physical sense—but emotional danger was a different story.

Because if she wasn't careful, he could make inroads on her heart.

The very reason she was on edge.

Nick, on the other hand, seemed relaxed as he cut up tomatoes, sliced a red onion, and sprinkled cheese and croutons on the lettuce, all with surprising dexterity.

When he finished, he angled the bowl toward her and grinned. "Voilà. A masterpiece. I hope your spaghetti lives up to my culinary pièce de résistance."

At his exaggerated and very bad French accent, a giggle slipped out too fast for her to stifle—but she sobered when he did a double take. "What's wrong?"

"Nothing." His eyes warmed. "In fact, you should laugh more often. It makes your face come alive."

Heat rose on her cheeks, and she turned toward the refrigerator. Stuck her head in the freezer. Maybe the cold air would banish her flush. "I, uh, think I have a package of garlic bread in here." She took her time rummaging around, but at last she emerged with the small loaf. "Success. Why don't you set another place at the counter?" That would get him a few feet farther away.

"You got it." At her direction, he pulled another plate from one cabinet and retrieved more utensils and a napkin from the drawer she pointed to. "What about a water glass?"

"I'll get one for you." She stopped stirring the noodles she'd dumped into the pot of boiling water, opened the adjacent cabinet, and stood on tiptoe to reach for the glass.

When she turned back to hand it to him, he quickly redirected his gaze from her midriff to the tumbler.

Shoot.

Her cropped T-shirt must have crept up when she'd reached for the glass.

Nick's reaction was why she never wore it in public.

She tugged it down as she handed him the glass. "I'm sorry I don't have the air on. I usually only run it during heat waves." Maybe she could redirect his attention.

"No worries." He swallowed. Cleared his throat. "This is much more comfortable than the sauna under that tent today." He went back to setting his place. "If I'd known we were going to eat together, I'd have brought red wine. It would be perfect with this meal."

Her gaze flicked to the cabinet at the end of the counter.

There was a bottle of cab in there, a Christmas gift from a client that she'd been saving for a special occasion.

Did this qualify?

Maybe.

After all, she'd never before invited a man to share a meal

with her here—even if this dinner was impromptu.

And if Nick wanted wine, the least she could do was offer him some after all the trouble he'd gone to on her behalf today.

"As a matter of fact, you'll find a bottle over there. Bottom shelf." She indicated the cabinet. "Help yourself."

He hesitated. "Will you join me?"

"Yes. Why don't you open it while I get us wine glasses and put the food out?"

He did as she asked, then joined her at the table, pouring each of them a glass. "Everything smells delicious. Your grandmother must have been an excellent cook."

"She was."

"Was she Italian?"

"Not even one percent. But she loved to experiment with dishes from other countries, even though she spent her whole life in a tiny town in southern Missouri."

When she mentioned the name, he shook his head. "I've never heard of it."

"Not many people have." She took a bite of salad.

"Is that where you grew up?"

"Yes."

"I always envied people who came from small towns. I've spent all of my life in big cities. I was born in Denver."

"Small-town life has some advantages—but not many opportunities."

"I suppose that's true. How's the salad?"

"Surprisingly good."

His lips quirked. "I think I'm insulted."

"Sorry. To be honest, you don't look like the type of man who'd spend much time in the kitchen."

"As a bachelor, learning the basics is a matter of survival."

He kept the conversation flowing while they ate, and as the meal progressed the tension in her shoulders ebbed.

In fact, by the time the last crust of garlic bread had been eaten, she was totally mellow. And her relaxed state wasn't due to the single glass of wine she'd downed, either. Nick got all the credit. The man was super easy to be with.

As she wiped her lips on her napkin and set it beside her plate, she gave him a rueful look. "I'm afraid I can't offer you dessert. I don't keep sweets in the house. They're too much of a temptation."

He finished off his wine. Cocked his head. "I have a suggestion. Why don't we pay a visit to Ted Drewes?"

The iconic frozen custard stand that was a St. Louis institution?

Tempting.

"I do have a weakness for their strawberry concretes."

"I'm a caramel man myself, but I haven't been there in years. You game?"

"I don't know." She took a sip of water. "It's getting pretty late." And spending any more time with a man who could make her wish for things she'd long ago written off might not be wise.

Nick twisted his wrist. Blinked at his watch. "How can it be nine-thirty already?"

"Time flies and all that."

He treated her to another smile, displaying a killer dimple. How had she not noticed that before? "Tonight *has* been fun. And this is the peak time for Ted Drewes on a Friday night. The place will be packed."

That was true.

Plus, a frozen custard would be a perfect end to a very enjoyable evening. And what could be the harm? A visit to an ice cream stand wasn't like bar-hopping or going dancing or sitting with him in a darkened movie theater.

Quashing her lingering doubts, she nodded. "I'm sold. Give me a minute to grab my purse."

"No rush. I'll clear the table and load the dishwasher."

"Why don't I do that first?"

As she started to reach for the plates, he stopped her with a touch on her arm. "Let me. That way we won't have any delays in getting our treat."

The warmth of his fingers seeped into her skin—and sent her pulse off the scale.

As treats went, it didn't get much better than a caring touch from a handsome man.

Even if men were off limits.

"Okay." She took a step back, breaking the contact, then fled to the safety of her room.

After shutting the door, she leaned back against it and took several long, deep breaths.

She needed to get a grip.

Nick seemed to be a nice man. Kind, considerate, well-read, an excellent conversationalist. And in another world, she might let herself get carried away by all sorts of romantic fantasies.

But she couldn't do that in her world. Not with her history.

So she'd eat her frozen custard, enjoy what remained of this evening, and then keep her distance as much as the forced proximity of the art center project allowed.

Because the last thing in the world she should do was encourage any interest he might have in her.

Nevertheless, before she rejoined him she ran a brush through her hair and applied a touch of lipstick.

Not for Nick, of course. She just wanted to look presentable in public.

That was her story—and she was sticking to it.

* * *

As Friday evenings went, this was turning out to be one of his better ones of late—despite the heat in Laura's unairconditioned apartment.

Nick picked up his jacket as he waited for her to return.

Money had to be the reason she didn't often turn on her air. What else could it be?

But he'd accept another dinner invitation from her in a heartbeat, no matter the temperature.

Unfortunately, the odds of a repeat performance seemed marginal at best. While she'd seemed to enjoy their dinner once she relaxed, she'd made it clear she wasn't in the market for romance.

Unless he could change her mind.

"All set."

He turned toward the short hall, and his spirits ticked up a bit. Her slightly breathless voice and the touch of lipstick she'd applied could be signs she found him appealing.

"I'm parked right in front." He crossed to the door and opened it. Once she locked it, he followed her down the stairs.

Her step faltered when she spotted his car. "Is that yours?" She motioned toward the low-slung red Porsche—which was thankfully still parked where he'd left it. And intact.

"Yes."

"Nice." She picked up her pace again while she gave the sports car a once-over.

"It was a splurge." And a far cry from the utilitarian pickup she drove, as she'd no doubt concluded. "Also a bit out of character for me." Somehow it seemed important to clarify that he didn't make a habit of being wildly extravagant.

"We all deserve an occasional splurge. Everyone should enjoy the fruits of their labors." There was no envy or self-pity in her tone, nor any indication she resented the fact that her own financial situation wasn't yet secure enough to allow for such luxuries.

"What was *your* last splurge?" The question slipped out as he opened the passenger door.

She stilled for a nanosecond, then flashed him a smile as she slid onto the seat. "This trip to Ted Drewes."

He let it rest at that, and stayed with innocuous topics as they made the short drive to Ted Drewes.

As always, the lines stretched nearly into the street and parking was at a premium. A good-natured crowd of families, couples young and old, and groups of teenagers milled about, and a stretch limo was pulled up to the curb.

It took him two passes to find a parking spot, and only then because someone happened to pull out as he was approaching.

"This must be your lucky night." Laura sent him a smile.

"I guess it is." In more ways than one.

By the time he turned off the ignition and circled the car, she was already on her feet and closing the door.

"Oh." Her brow crinkled as she tucked her hair behind her ear. "Were you going to get my door?"

"That was my plan."

"Sorry. I'm used to doing everything for myself. But I appreciate the thought."

"No worries, as long as I didn't offend you."

Twin creases dented her brow. "Why would I be offended?"

He shrugged. "I've run into a few women who made it clear they considered men who opened doors and held chairs to be chauvinists." Like Lauren. Which was one of the many reasons—albeit a lesser one—that she was history. "But my mother trained me well, and those are hard habits to break."

"No offense taken. I appreciate good manners." She waved toward the stand. "Shall we join the line?"

He followed her over, and once they had their treats in hand they returned to his car and leaned against the back while they ate.

All too fast, however, the custard was gone. Meaning he'd have to take her home and end this pleasant evening.

But perhaps, if his luck held, there'd be another one down the road.

He called up a smile and took her empty cardboard cup. "We made short work of these."

"Yes. And on top of all that pasta too." She shook her head. "This was not a heart-healthy meal. And it wasn't too great for the waistline either."

"Like you have to worry about that."

Despite his joking tone, a flicker of distress flashed in her irises and bad vibes wafted his way.

Uh-oh.

Apparently he'd made a faux pas.

Better fix that. Fast.

"Did I say something wrong?"

She offered him a smile that was a little too bright. "No. Of course not."

Maybe not, but for whatever reason his comment had struck a nerve with her.

"Let me clarify anyway. I meant that as a compliment. You look very fit."

Her lips flattened. "You mean skinny."

The way she said the word, it sounded like a pejorative.

"Is being thin a bad thing?"

"Not necessarily." She dipped her head and toed a piece of loose gravel on the pavement. "But some people equate thin with scrawny. Which isn't very…appealing."

He stared at her.

Laura thought she was unattractive? With a figure that would be the envy of any model?

Impossible.

"Do you seriously think you're unappealing?"

She took a deep breath. "I don't think I'm ugly, if that's what you mean, but people look at more than a face."

"You mean guys." Because it was sounding more and more like some jerk had dinged her self-image. Big time.

Maybe somebody she'd dated after her husband died?

She lifted one shoulder. "I'm not interested in dating again anyway, so it doesn't matter."

"It matters to me." He kept his voice quiet but firm.

She studied him. "Why?"

Because I'd like to convince you to start *dating again.*

But he kept that to himself. The last thing he wanted to do was spook her.

"I don't like to see people underestimate themselves." He chose his words with care. "I'm a guy, and believe me, you were a knockout in that little black dress you wore today. And you don't look too shabby in those shorts and that T-shirt, either."

"Right." She huffed out a humorless laugh. "I guess that's why the only guy who gave me a second look at the party was drunk."

He sucked in a breath, anger coiling inside him.

Someone had hurt this woman. Badly.

"No one who looks like you do should have any doubt about

her attractiveness." He tried hard to keep his voice calm and steady. "I can only conclude that some jerk did a number on you."

He braced, expecting her to shut down. Send a clear message that he'd overstepped.

But she didn't.

Instead, she tucked her hair behind her ear. Folded her arms. Sniffed. "It's a long story, Nick."

So there *was* a story.

"I figured it might be." He filled his lungs. "You know, sometimes it helps to talk about bad stuff."

"Sometimes. But not tonight."

Despite the temptation to press her, he resisted. Pushing would only backfire.

Someday, if he earned her trust, she'd tell him her story.

"Let me get rid of these and I'll take you home." He lifted the empty cups, strode across the parking lot, and pitched them in the trash can.

When he returned, she was waiting by the passenger door.

Her quiet, heartfelt thank-you when he opened it for her tightened his throat.

Such a simple courtesy would only evoke such sincere appreciation if a person had known very few of them.

Anger once again flared in his gut.

Whatever scars Laura bore were deep.

On the brief ride home he tried to keep the conversation upbeat and flowing, but the mood had changed.

When he parked in front of her apartment, she remained in her seat while he circled the car, his worry meter spiking as he gave the poorly lit area a scan. "You don't wander around here at night, do you?" He kept an eye on the surroundings as he pulled her door open.

"No. But it's a safe neighborhood."

He let that pass, but stayed close while he walked her to the entrance and up the dimly lit stairway to her door.

"Thank you again for a lovely evening." She fitted her key in the lock and opened her door.

"The thanks are all mine. The meal was delicious, and the company was even better." If her ego needed boosting, he was more than happy to do his part.

In fact, he'd like nothing better than to demonstrate just how attracted he was to her.

With any other woman, he wouldn't hesitate to follow that inclination—but if he moved too fast with Laura, he could shoot himself in the foot.

Yet how could he walk away without giving her some concrete proof that she was an attractive, desirable woman? Just a simple gesture, but one that would send a strong message.

She dropped her keys into her purse and angled back toward him. "Good night, Nick. Sweet dreams."

"Guaranteed." Gaze locked on hers, he slowly lifted his hand. Fingered a lock of her oh-so-soft hair.

Her breath hitched—but she didn't move.

After a few moments, he released the strands, letting his knuckles gently graze her cheek as he withdrew his hand. Then he turned and forced himself to walk away.

Before his shaky self-control snapped and he did something he could come to regret.

5

"You haven't mentioned our friend, Nick, lately." Sam helped herself to another loaded potato skin.

Ignoring her best friend's comment, Laura surveyed the bar as the rowdy Saturday night crowd shouted to be heard over the loud music. The cacophony was ear-splitting. Thankfully they'd managed to snag a bar table off to one side, out of the center of the action. "Why in the world did you pick this place? The noise is giving me a headache."

"It's a hot spot."

"It's a meat market."

Sam shrugged. "Same difference. So how's Nick?"

Expelling a sigh, Laura shook her head. "Do you ever give up?"

"Nope." She took a bite of the potato skin, talking as she chewed. "That's the problem with you, you know. You've given up on men."

"Why do we always end up talking about men?"

"Because good friends should discuss important things. And men fall into that category."

Laura angled away from the boisterous crowd. "Sam. Your marriage was a disaster. Right?"

"Right."

"So why do you want to find another man and repeat the mistake?"

"You are way too cynical. Just because we married two losers doesn't mean all men are bad. There are plenty of good guys out there who would love to meet a wholesome, hard-working woman like you and a street-smart, sassy woman like me. And I bet if we found the right ones, they'd treat us like queens."

Images of Nick from their unexpected evening together last night flashed through her mind, but Laura quashed them at once. She was *not* going to let Sam's ongoing hunt for the perfect man stir up silly romantic fantasies.

"Maybe. But I, for one, am not willing to take the chance. Speaking of men, though, how did your date turn out last night? Who was it this week? The accountant?"

"No. Jay, the engineer. It was okay." Sam picked up another potato skin. "We went to a movie, stopped for a drink, had a few laughs. You know, the usual."

"No. I don't know."

"You could if you wanted to."

"I *don't* want to."

"That's the problem. You *should* want to. This may not be your scene." Sam waved the potato skin over the crowd. "But there are other ways to meet men. I'm not saying you need to date twice a week, but twice a month would be nice. Heck, at this point I'd settle for twice a year."

"I don't have time for dates. Besides, I don't have your skill when it comes to meeting men. How do you manage to find all the guys you go out with, anyway?"

"It's elementary, my dear Laura. I look. You don't. Even when there's a fine specimen right under your nose, do you notice? No. So tell me how it's going with Nick."

"Why are you so fixated on him?"

"He's the only man you've seen regularly in years."

"I see him because we're working on the same project. It's a professional relationship." Or it had been, until last night.

"You mention him a lot." Sam picked a piece of bacon off her potato skin. Popped it in her mouth. "That tells me you're interested in him beyond working hours."

"No, I'm not."

"Yes, you are. So when did you see him last?"

Uh-oh.

Laura took a sip of her iced tea.

She didn't keep much from Sam, and at some point she'd dish about last night's impromptu dinner. But at the moment she was still processing the—

"What aren't you telling me?" Sam stopped eating.

Laura let out a slow breath.

This was the downside to having a best friend. They learned to read you.

And maybe that was okay. Maybe Sam could help her sort through the strange mix of emotions that were muddling her brain.

She took a potato skin and plucked off a green onion. "As a matter of fact, I saw him last night."

"Last night, as in after work?" Interest sparked in Sam's eyes.

"Yes."

"You've been holding out on me."

"It was no big deal. And it wasn't planned. He kind of came to my rescue at the arts center groundbreaking party yesterday." She gave her a quick recap of the drunk incident and the dropped mirror and Nick's trip to her apartment to return it. "I'd just made a batch of spaghetti sauce, and after he'd gone to all that trouble, I thought it was only polite to invite him to stay for dinner."

Sam carefully set her potato skin on her plate, pushed it aside, and linked her fingers on the table. "Let me get this straight. You invited a man to dinner."

"Yes."

"Well, hallelujah!" She looked up and lifted her palms to the heavens. "Did he stay?"

"Yes."

"Double hallelujah. What happened after dinner?"

"He took me to Ted Drewes for dessert."

Sam's face lit up. "He extended the evening. Excellent. Did you have fun?"

"Not at first. I was pretty nervous."

"That's to be expected. You haven't dated for a while."

"Like in fourteen years."

"Well, there you go. You're just out of practice. Do you think he'll ask you out again?"

"He didn't ask me out *this* time."

Sam waved that aside. "You know what I mean. Do you think he enjoyed the evening?"

Another image flitted through her mind, of the banked fire in Nick's eyes as he'd played with her hair for that sizzling moment before he'd left.

She took a steadying breath. Wadded her paper cocktail napkin in her fingers. "Yes. But I'm not ready to dive into a relationship."

Sam snorted. "Honey, you're past ready. You're ripe."

At that pithy comment, a chuckle bubbled up inside her.

Not everyone appreciated Sam's blunt, earthy honesty, but she'd been a true friend and lifesaver during the rough times. No one could have been more steadfast, loyal, and supportive than the woman sitting across from her.

"I'm not sure I'd go that far." Laura smiled.

"I would. So tell me what he looks like. I assume you've taken a better inventory by now."

"You know I'm not good at describing people."

"Well, does he look like anyone here?" Sam waved her hand over the room.

Laura scanned the crowd around them. "No. It's hard for me to see resemblances. Besides, no one here is—" She blinked.

Was that Nick on the other side of the room, leaning against the bar?

"What's going on?" Sam followed her line of sight.

It *was* him.

Heart stuttering, she shifted around on her stool until her back was to the room. "He's here."

"Nick?"

"Yes."

"Where?" Sam craned her neck.

"Will you please stop staring?"

Sam ignored her. "Point him out to me."

"No." She hunched lower.

As her so-called friend continued to peruse the bar, Laura grabbed her purse.

The instant the milling crowd configured itself to provide cover for an escape, she was out of here.

* * *

If he never attended another bachelor party, it would be too soon.

Nick leaned against the bar, swirling the ice in his gin and tonic and plotting his escape.

Funny.

Once upon a time, he'd enjoyed the singles scene.

Now the whole bar-hopping, let's-make-small-talk treadmill was boring.

Truth be told, he'd rather spend his Saturday nights at home, like Jack did, with a wife and family who were more interested in his love and affection than in his sports car or the fancy dinners he could provide at high-end restaurants.

He sipped his drink and tossed another handful of peanuts into his mouth.

Too bad a sit-down meal wasn't on the agenda tonight. A restaurant would be quieter, and his eardrums would welcome even a few decibels less noise.

Unfortunately, the bachelor party was only hitting bars.

He gave the room a scan, his gaze connecting with a redhead's on the far side. She was attractive enough in a flamboyant sort of way, and when she smiled at him he smiled back—an autopilot move he regretted at once. No way did he want to encourage *any* unwanted advances tonight.

But maybe she wasn't on the make, since she already had a companion. A woman with strawberry blond hair.

Hair the same color and length as Laura's.

He squinted at her back.

Could it be her?

Hard to tell, but the odds had to be minuscule. Laura didn't seem like the type who'd frequent singles bars.

The redhead continued to smile at him even after the other woman leaned toward her intently, the rigid line of her shoulders spelling stress in capital letters—and looking suddenly familiar.

He straightened up

Maybe it *was* Laura.

And what could it hurt to find out? Worst case, he was wrong.

At which point he could beat a hasty retreat.

But if it *was* her, this encounter would be the highlight of his night.

He wove through the crowd, and the closer he got the more certain he was that the woman was Laura.

A suspicion he confirmed when he reached their table and caught a glimpse of her profile. "Hello, Laura. I thought it was you."

She cleared her throat. Flashed him a quick smile. "Hi, Nick."

Silence, filled only by the pulsing beat of the music…until the redhead stepped in.

"I don't believe we've met. I'm Sam Reynolds." She held out her hand.

Nick gave her fingers a firm squeeze as he introduced himself, then cocked his head. "Are you certain we haven't met? Your voice sounds familiar."

"We've spoken." Sam grinned. "I answered the phone at Laura's office the day you called looking for her."

Nick winced. "Then I think I owe you an apology. As I recall, I was a little abrupt that day."

"You were, but I survived."

"Maybe we can start over. After all, Laura gave me a second chance, and I was even less friendly to her." He called up his most engaging grin.

"Done. Would you like to join us?"

Laura gave her a side-eye, which Sam ignored.

"Yes, I would. Thanks." Nick commandeered an empty stool from an adjacent table and wedged it in next to Laura's. Close enough to get a whiff of the fresh fragrance that wafted from her hair every time she moved.

"Help yourself to a potato skin." Sam pushed the plate toward him.

"Thanks, but I've had my fill of bar food tonight."

"I hope we're not taking you away from your friends." Sam waved a hand toward the throng.

"No. It's a bachelor party, and if you've seen one, you've seen them all. I was about to make my excuses, anyway."

"Good. Then you can stay awhile. Isn't that great, Laura?" Sam gave her an elbow nudge.

Soft color stole over her cheeks. "Yes. Great." But she didn't sound any too happy about him joining their party.

Not that he intended to let her lack of enthusiasm deter him.

"Can I buy you ladies a drink?"

"Thanks. I'll have another tonic water." Sam finished off the one she was drinking.

"Laura?"

"I'm still working on this iced tea."

Nick signaled to the waitress and relayed the order before resuming the conversation. "So what brings you two to this mecca for swinging singles?"

"What do you think?" Humor glinted in Sam's irises. "We're looking for men. Are you available?"

"Sam!"

At Laura's horrified admonition, Nick chuckled. "Your friend here doesn't pull any punches, does she?" He tipped his head toward Sam.

Laura glowered at her. "She can be very direct. But that's *not* why we're here. At least *I'm* not here for that reason. Sam picked this place."

"I'm glad she did. Otherwise there wouldn't have been anyone to rescue me from the bachelor party. And to answer your question, Sam, yes, I am." Out of the corner of his eye, he caught a glimpse of his group heading toward the door. "Would you excuse me for a minute? I think the bachelor party is moving on and I want to let them know I'm peeling off."

"Sure." Sam took the glass the server delivered. "We're not going anywhere."

Nick hesitated. Turned to Laura. "Will you wait?" Because in light of the tension radiating from her, he wouldn't put it past her to bolt the second he stepped away.

The color that crept over her cheeks told him his take had been spot-on.

"She'll wait." Sam raised her glass. "Guaranteed."

"I owe you." He gave her a thumbs-up.

"I'll remember that."

He flexed his lips. "I'm sure you will. I'll be back in a minute."

Picking up his pace, he wove through the crowd.

He had no doubt Sam would find a way to keep Laura at the table.

But rather than press his luck, he intended to get back there as fast as possible.

* * *

The moment Nick was out of earshot Laura turned to Sam. "I can't believe you did that."

"What?" Sam gave her the innocent act.

"You know what. First you invite him to join us, then you ask personal questions. It was embarrassing."

"Why? He didn't seem to mind. And you should thank me. Now you know for sure he's available. No girlfriend or significant other in the wings. The field is wide open."

"Available and interested are two different things."

"Laura." Sam leaned closer to her. "The man came over here tonight to say hello to you. He initiated an encounter. Then he agreed to join us. Plus, when he looks at you his eyes get soft. Trust me, the man is interested."

"Maybe the woman isn't."

"She is."

Trying to avoid the truth with Sam was an exercise in futility.

"Fine. Maybe she is." Laura traced a bead of sweat down her glass with a shaky finger. "But she's also nervous."

"Why do you think that is?" Sam studied her.

"Because I haven't been around a man in a social setting for a very long time."

"Wrong answer, kiddo. Not just any man could unsettle you. Only Nick. Because you're attracted to him, and that's a threat to your insulated existence. You want my two cents? Go for it. He's not only hot, he's got personality and a sense of humor."

Before she could respond, Nick rejoined them. "Did you miss me?"

"Oh, were you gone?"

At Sam's feigned surprise, Nick grinned. "That'll keep a guy's ego in check."

As the two of them indulged in a bit more good-natured banter, Laura's spirits deflated.

Sam was so at ease with Nick, while she was a mass of vibrating nerves. She couldn't even think of one witty remark to add to the repartee.

Dipping her chin, she stirred her tea. Except there was nothing to stir, really. The ice had melted, washing out the color.

What an apt analogy for her life. Most days she felt like a pale image of the woman she used to be, before bad decisions had taken a huge emotional toll and left her—

"…so I'll leave you two to carry on."

Her attention snapped back to the conversation as Sam slid off her stool.

"Where are you going?" A thread of panic wove through her voice.

"Home to bed. I have to show a house early tomorrow morning and I want to be thinking clearly when I meet the client. He's only in town for the weekend, so it's now or never for the sale. Nick, it was nice meeting you." Sam held her hand out to him.

He stood and took it. "Likewise. Can I walk you to your car?"

"Thanks, but I'm parked next to the door. Besides, I just spotted someone I know at the bar and I want to say hello. But do me a favor and walk Laura to hers when she leaves. She's at the far end of the lot."

"Already in my plans."

"Good man." Sam gave an approving nod.

Laura frowned.

Why were they talking about her as if she wasn't here?

She straightened in her seat. "For the record, I'm quite capable of taking care of myself."

"Of course you are." Sam waved at someone across the room. "But if you're with a gentleman, let him act like one. Good night, Nick."

As Sam sauntered toward the bar, Nick retook his seat. "I like her. Her candor is very…charming."

Laura snorted. "I can think of another word for it."

His lips twitched. "Don't knock her good intentions. She graciously bowed out, leaving you alone with me, and she arranged for you to get to your car safely. What more could you ask?"

That she butt out, for one thing.

But Laura left that unsaid.

She picked up her purse from the table. Played with the clasp. "Look, you don't have to keep me company. I was thinking about heading home anyway. This isn't my style."

"I'm not finding the atmosphere very appealing, either. As for keeping you company, I wouldn't have come over here if I hadn't wanted to spend time with you."

"That's what Sam said." She glanced at her friend, who was now carrying on an animated conversation with an attractive man at the bar.

"Sam has excellent insights. But I'm not sure you're happy about me being here. You seem stressed."

"I'm not stressed." A definite stretch of the truth.

Nick reached over and captured her fingers, gentling his voice when he spoke. "Your hands are trembling." His thumb moved to her wrist. "Your pulse is rapid. Your respiration is shallow. With any other woman, I might attribute those reactions to something pleasant. But you're just plain scared, aren't you?"

Sucking in a breath, she snatched her hand away.

Speaking of excellent insights.

Nick blew out a breath. "Sorry. I overstepped. So before I shoot myself in the other foot, let me change the subject. Jack and his wife, Melissa, are throwing a pre-Fourth-of-July barbecue next Saturday. Would you like to go with me?"

Her pulse tripped.

Nick was asking her on a date? A real one, not an

unexpected, spur-of-the-moment get-together?

A strange combination of yearning and fear surged through her. "I, uh, work on Saturdays."

"All day?" He signaled for the server to bring the bill.

"Sometimes. I may have more employees now, but I'm a one-person show when it comes to management. Saturdays are when I get caught up on the books. Besides, I'm going home for a long weekend over Fourth of July, so I need to make up that time."

"We could go to the party late. After you finish working."

He was persistent—and making it hard to say no.

And what harm could come from going? On the plus side, maybe if she had a few more social engagements Sam would get off her back.

She glanced toward the bar again, just in time to see Sam heading for the door on the arm of the man she'd been talking to. Her best friend never seemed at a loss for male companionship.

If Sam could go out with a host of different men, maybe *she* should agree to go out with one.

Taking a deep breath, she turned back to Nick—and took the plunge. "Okay."

For a moment he seemed taken aback, but he recovered fast. "Great. I'll call you this week to firm up the plans."

"That'll work."

The server swung by. "This bill's already been taken care of, sir."

"I had a feeling Sam would do that before she left." Laura withdrew her keys from her purse. "And I need to go too. It's been a long day."

"I'll walk you out." He stood.

"Honestly, that's not necessary. Sam tends to be overprotective."

"A promise is a promise. Shall we?" He motioned toward the door.

Rather than argue, she slung her purse over her shoulder and wove through the crowd toward the exit, leaving Nick to fall in behind.

As she stepped into the warm night air, Laura drew a deep breath of the fresh air. "I hate these kinds of places."

"Then why are you here?"

"Sam likes them. She drags me along now and then, hoping to enhance my social life." She tried for a joking tone.

Nick's was serious when he responded. "If your social life is lacking, I have to believe it's by choice."

They were creeping into personal territory, just as they had last night at Ted Drewes. And she wasn't ready to go there yet.

"The business keeps me busy." She picked up her pace toward her car.

But when they reached it, Nick leaned against the side and folded his arms, as if he was in no hurry to leave.

"Thanks for walking me out." She opened her door.

"No problem." He remained where he was.

"Well…" She tightened her grip on her keys. "I should be going."

A few seconds ticked by. "May I tell you something, Laura?"

In this dimly lit corner of the lot, it was impossible to read the nuances in his features. But the serious note in his voice put her on alert. "I guess so."

"If you were any other woman, I'd move in for a kiss right now. But I'm not going to do that, because the last thing I want to do is scare you off. I hope someday you'll welcome a kiss, but I can wait. And I can also promise you this. I will never hurt you."

Pressure built in her throat at his quiet pledge.

She didn't doubt his sincerity. It was clear he meant what he said.

But hurts happened despite promises. Even with people you thought you knew well.

That's why it was safer to keep your distance from relationships.

"I appreciate those words, but I don't want to give you false hope. I have major trust issues." It was only fair to be as honest with him as he was being with her.

"I already figured that out. And I'm a patient man. So for now, this will suffice."

As he'd done last night, he reached over. Fingered her hair. Brushed the back of his hand across her cheek, his touch featherlight. Then he straightened up. "Good night, Laura. I'll call you this week about the barbecue."

"Okay." Her response came out in a hoarse croak.

He took a couple of steps back, but waited until she slid behind the wheel, locked her door, and started the engine to lift a hand in farewell and melt into the night.

Leaving her wanting more than a mere touch of her hair—and battling the fear that was her legacy.

6

When her cell began to vibrate on her nightstand at…Laura propped open her eyes and peered at her watch…seven-fifteen the next morning, she stifled a groan.

After her restless night, another hour of shut-eye would have been welcome.

But if someone was calling her at this hour on a Sunday, it must be important.

Rolling onto her side, she fumbled for the phone. Squinted at the screen.

Sam.

Of course.

Her best friend no doubt wanted a full report on the success of her not-so-subtle matchmaking efforts last night.

She put the phone to her ear, stifling a yawn. "Morning."

A beat ticked by. "Did I wake you?"

"Yep."

"You're always up by six. And you always go to the early church service. Tell me you slept in because you stayed out late with Nick."

"Sorry to disappoint you, but no. I left not long after you did. By the way, who was your friend at the bar?" Trying to keep track of Sam's ever-changing cast of admirers was a losing battle, but maybe the question would distract her.

"Just a guy from my office. We've gone out a few times, had some laughs. Nothing serious. He walked me to my car, and we said goodnight. I have an early appointment today, remember? But *you* don't. Why did your evening end so soon? Did you clam up or do something to discourage Nick?"

"No. I just said I was ready to call it a night."

"Wonderful." Sam huffed out a breath. "If you don't give the man some encouragement, he'll lose interest."

She pushed herself upright and wedged her pillow behind her. "I don't think he's losing interest."

A beat ticked by. "Meaning?"

"He asked me out for next weekend."

"Yes! Please tell me you're going."

"I'm going. It's a barbecue at his partner's house, so there will be plenty of people around. It should be safe."

"From what?"

Laura took a deep breath. "Getting too cozy, if you know what I mean."

"I know what you mean. But why are you worried about that? Did he put some moves on you last night?"

"He didn't kiss me or anything."

"Not even an attempt?"

"No." She plucked at a loose thread on the blanket. "He said he wanted to, but I think he knows I'm running scared."

"Huh. That's impressive. If he was willing to forego a moment of pleasure for a greater payoff down the road, he's seriously interested. I like a man who has self-control and smarts."

"He did touch my hair, though. And my face."

"And you let him?" Incredulity raised Sam's pitch.

"Yes."

"Well, that's a start."

"But that's the thing. I'm not sure I *want* to start anything."

"So you didn't like it when he touched you."

Leave it to Sam to dig into the nitty-gritty.

"I did like it. And to be honest, part of me was sorry that's all he did. Which is weird, considering how careful I've been to avoid entanglements."

"Laura. You've been living in an emotional cave for a decade. Frankly, I'm surprised your pent-up hormones haven't revolted before now. I understand why you want to move slowly, and believe it or not I think that's smart. But you're past due for *some* movement."

She bunched the sheet in her free hand. "I hear what you're saying, and I don't disagree in principle. But in practice, I could get hurt again."

"Not every relationship ends in hurt." When Sam continued, her voice was subdued—for Sam. "You've never said much about your marriage, and I've always respected your boundaries. But it doesn't take a genius to do the math. When we met, you were heartbreakingly sad. Plus, I saw what Joe did to you the night you left him. I know walking away was tough for you, but it was the right thing to do. Randy may have been a bum, but he never physically hurt me."

Laura closed her eyes. This was a part of her life she'd never shared with anyone in detail. But Sam had seen enough to get the general lay of the land. And maybe talking about it now, after all these years, could have some benefits. Help her deal with the lingering pain and regret and guilt. "Joe wasn't always like that. He changed. For a long time, I thought it was because of me."

"Is that what he told you? That his problems were your fault?" Indignation scored Sam's voice.

Yeah, he had. And she'd bought into that guilt trip for too long.

"Yes. But I eventually realized he was sick and needed professional help. Whenever I suggested that, though, it infuriated him. That's when he started expressing his anger with violence, and I was too scared to push back. In hindsight, though, maybe I should have."

"Or not. From what I saw the night you walked out, you might not be around if you'd pushed."

Sam had a point.

"That's history now anyway. But people do change. I thought I knew Joe, and look what happened. How can I ever trust my judgment about a man again when I was so wrong about him?"

A sigh came over the line. "I wish I had a glib answer for you, but I don't. All I can tell you is that as far as I can see, your judgment is sound. Still, commitment does involves risk. Relationships don't come with a money-back guarantee or a lifetime warranty. You just have to use all the information at your disposal and then take your best shot."

Laura released the sheet. Smoothed out the wrinkles. "You're always the voice of common sense. What would I do without you?"

"Survive. Because you are one strong lady."

"I haven't been feeling all that strong lately. Nick's thrown me for a loop."

"Which isn't a bad thing if it nudges you out of your rut. But you don't have to rush into a relationship. Set a pace that's comfortable for you, and if he's a man worth having, he'll follow your cues. And speaking of loops—keep me in yours. I want a detailed report on your barbecue outing. Capisce?"

"I don't speak Italian."

"Neither do I. So make sure the report is in English. Now I

have to run or my client will be champing at the bit. Talk to you soon, kiddo."

When they ended the call, Laura set the phone beside her. Stared at the wall across from the bed.

Talking to Sam was always helpful.

And as usual, her best friend was right. She *was* in a rut. One that kept her on the sidelines of life, watching the parade pass by instead of being part of it.

That was safer, for sure. Being an observer carried no risk. Nor did participating in romance vicariously through novels and rom-com movies.

But from-afar participation was a pale facsimile of the cavalcade of emotions that had swept through her when Nick touched her hair in the dim light of the parking lot last night as electricity pinged around them.

And if that simple gesture could set her heart aflutter and shut down her lungs, what would a kiss do?

As the temperature in the room spiked, she threw back the covers.

If this kept up, she might have to cave and turn on the air.

But one thing for sure.

There would be no more sleep this morning.

* * *

By Friday, it appeared that her report to Sam on the barbecue was going to be super brief.

Because Nick hadn't called to finalize the arrangements.

Laura gave the pad of paper beside her laptop a glum scan.

All she had to show for the past half hour of so-called work was a series of unproductive doodles.

This was why she avoided relationships. They were rife with disappointment. And letting your emotional state be tied to a man's whims was a recipe for disaster. Been there, done that, not going there again.

It was probably better that Nick had let her down early on, rather than after she became invested in—

The cell at her elbow began to vibrate, and she put it to her ear without checking the screen. "Taylor Landscaping."

"Laura, it's Nick. I'm sorry I haven't been in touch all week."

She took a steadying breath as her heart skipped a beat. "No problem." The reassurance sounded stiff even to her own ears.

"I would have called sooner, but it's been crazy. I'm afraid I'm going to have to renege on the barbecue. There isn't much that would make me break our date, but my dad had what everyone thought was a stroke on Wednesday morning. I flew to Denver on the first flight I could get, and I haven't had a spare moment since then."

A wave of guilt crashed over her, and she closed her eyes.

Nick hadn't forgotten about their date. Nor had he intentionally disappointed her.

"I'm so sorry. How is he doing?"

"Better. It turned out to be a TIA. But I'm going to hang around until Sunday."

"Of course."

"I'm really sorry about tomorrow night."

"Don't be. Family comes first."

"Thanks for understanding. I'll call you when I get back and we'll put another date on the books. Don't work too hard this weekend."

"I'll try not to."

Once they said their goodbyes, Laura set the cell back beside her.

The good news was that she'd misread Nick's tardiness in following through on his promise to call. He did still want to see her.

The bad news was how she'd reacted when she'd thought he was brushing her off.

They hardly knew each other, and already she'd given him the power to hurt her.

That was *very* bad news.

Best plan?

Pull back until she decided how to proceed.

Trying to explain that to Nick without totally shutting the door could be tricky, though.

So she'd have to give that serious thought over the next few days and plan her strategy.

But by Monday afternoon, when his name flashed on her cell screen at a job site, she still hadn't come up with an ideal approach.

Pulse picking up, she moved away from a pile of compost and started with the most important topic once she greeted him. "How's your dad doing?"

"Much better. He's home, and grateful he had a warning rather than a full-fledged stroke. Medication and diet changes should be sufficient to control the risk of another episode. Now on to more pleasant topics. I can't re-create the barbecue, but I'd like to take you to dinner Wednesday night if you're free."

A few feet away, her crew dug into the compost pile, the earthy smell drifting her way as she gripped her phone tighter. "I'm sorry, I can't. Fourth of July is approaching fast, and if I want to take a four-day weekend I need to put in longer hours this week."

"But you have to eat. We could make it a quick dinner."

"This isn't the best week, Nick."

Several beats ticked by. "I could stop by one night for a late run to Ted Drewes." There was a tad of caution in his voice now.

"Not this week."

"Okay." But the frown in his voice said otherwise. "We can try again next week. I'll call you then."

She squeezed the phone tighter. Took a fortifying breath. "Nick, I think it's only fair to—"

"Hang on a sec." He spoke to someone else, the voices muffled, and when he returned he sounded distracted. "I have to run. Enjoy the holiday, and we'll talk next week."

So much for telling him about her concerns.

They said their goodbyes, and when the screen went dark Laura blew out a breath.

She'd certainly handled that well.

Not.

So next time he called she'd have to be more straightforward.

Until then, though, she wasn't going to let anything ruin her rare weekend visit home. And once she got there, she wouldn't have time to think about Nick. The Anderson Fourth of July gathering was legendary, drawing family from far and wide for what had become an annual family reunion. She'd missed several during her marriage to Joe, but none since. Nor would she miss any in the future.

As it turned out, she didn't have much time to dwell on Nick during the week, either. Her schedule these days was crazy. But after all the lean start-up years, no way was she going to complain about the volume of work.

When she finally slid behind the wheel of her truck on

Friday after work, her lips bowed.

Tomorrow morning she'd be on the road home. If she had to work a little more tonight at her apartment before shutting down for the holiday, so be it. She'd be rewarded with four glorious days of freedom.

Not surprisingly, her stomach rumbled as she put the key in the ignition. That's what happened when you worked through lunch. But with any luck she'd have a simple meal on the table within an hour.

Except luck was against her.

When she turned the key, the engine sputtered but didn't catch.

She tried again, with the same result. A third attempt was also futile.

Seriously?

Her truck might be old, but it was well-maintained and had always been reliable. How could it pick tonight to act up?

Laura scrubbed a hand down her face.

Sitting here lamenting over her situation wasn't going to change it. She'd just have to have the truck towed.

Fortunately her garage was still open, and her usual mechanic agreed to stay late to see if he could deal with the problem.

She cooled her heels for an hour and a half at the garage after they towed the truck in before Dave pushed through the door into the waiting area.

"Sorry, Laura." He wiped his hands on a greasy rag. "There's nothing I can do tonight. You've got a bad fuel pump, and we don't have any in stock. Fastest I could get one for you would probably be Tuesday."

Her spirits tanked.

But much as she'd like to vent, her ruined weekend wasn't Dave's fault.

She stood. "I appreciate you staying late tonight."

"No worries. I wish I could have gotten it up and running for you. But I can make it a priority on Tuesday."

"Thanks." Pressure built behind her eyes, and she blinked to clear her vision.

"Can I give you a lift home?"

She hesitated…but only for a moment. "If you wouldn't mind, that would be great. I only live a couple of miles from here, and it would save me calling an uber."

"You got it. Give me a minute to turn off the lights."

By the time Dave dropped her off at her apartment, it was nearly eight o'clock. Way past dinner time. But her appetite had vanished anyway.

Once she let herself into her unit, she set her laptop on the desk and dropped into one of the upholstered chairs, weighing her options.

Sam would have come to her rescue if she hadn't left today for a week's vacation in Chicago. But still. Asking for a ride to the office when your car broke down was one thing. Asking for a ride halfway across the state was another. Even if Sam was here, that would have been too much of an imposition.

It was possible she could book a rental car, but in all likelihood the affordable ones were already reserved for the holiday. And a bus was out of the question. With all the stops and time spent waiting for connections it wouldn't be worth the effort.

Conclusion?

Her long-awaited R&R was hosed.

The apartment grew dark, but she made no move to turn on any lights. The gloom suited her mood.

She ought to call her mom, though. Let her know she wouldn't be coming.

But Mom would be as disappointed as she was, and the two of them would end up in tears on the phone. It might be best to wait until she had her own dejection under control before she shared the downer news

Laura closed her eyes. Sighed.

Maybe her fairy godmother would appear with a coach. There were plenty of mice in this building to turn into footmen.

Her eyelids flickered, and just as she was on the verge of drifting off to sleep her cell began to vibrate in her pocket.

Pulling herself back from the brink of slumber, she blinked and put the phone to her ear. Mumbled a greeting.

"Laura?"

At Nick's voice, she jolted upright. "Yes. Hi."

"Hi back. You didn't sound like yourself for a minute."

"Sorry. I was half asleep."

"At nine-thirty? Are you sick?"

"No." She smothered a yawn. "Just tired."

"I'm glad you're taking a few days off. You need a break."

Her dour mood returned. "As it turns out, I'm not going to get one after all. My truck gave out. It's in the shop, and they won't be able to fix it until Tuesday."

"I'm so sorry." His voice softened in empathy. "I know how much you were looking forward to this. Is there any other way for you to get there?"

"Not unless my fairy godmother conjures up a coach. But I don't think I'm going to be as lucky as Cinderella."

A couple of beats passed. "You know, I don't have any plans for the weekend. I'm not exactly a fairy godmother, but I do have a working car. Why don't you let me drive you down?"

She blinked. Flipped on the light to make sure she was really awake. "Are you serious?"

"Yes."

"But…my family lives three hours from here."

"I like road trips."

Laura bit her lip.

She wanted to go home so badly she could taste it, but being up close and personal with Nick in a car for six hours, not to mention having him hang around her all weekend, didn't fit with her plan to keep a safe distance between them until she decided how, or if, to proceed with him. What was she supposed to do if—

"Hey." His gentle admonition interrupted her careening thoughts. "Don't overthink it. Just be grateful a chauffeur has magically appeared. And for the record, I'm not inviting myself to your family party. There must be a motel nearby where I can stay, and I'll settle for whatever time you can spare for me during the holiday."

This man was too good to be true.

Exactly the thing she was afraid of.

That, however, was a consideration for another day. Right now, she was too happy that her trip might be salvaged to let worries about the future dampen her spirits.

"If I accept your generous offer, you have to stay at the house. There's plenty of room. Besides, Mom would never forgive me if I relegated you to a motel."

"I wouldn't want to impose."

"You've got it backwards. I'm the one who would be imposing. Giving you a place to sleep would be small compensation in return for a ride home."

"There may be other compensations."

Uh-oh.

She stood. Started to pace. "Um…in the interest of full disclosure, we won't have a whole lot of privacy. And I don't want you to have unrealistic expectations."

"You mean you won't even feed me? I was hoping at minimum to get a home-cooked meal out of this."

Oh.

Maybe she'd read too much into his last comment.

She shook her head.

And she'd thought *men* had one-track minds on certain subjects.

"Of course we'll feed you. Mom puts on a Norman Rockwell spread on the Fourth—long tables covered with checkered cloths and loaded down with every kind of all-American food you can imagine."

"I'm hungry already. Would a ten o'clock departure work? I have a couple of things I need to do in the morning."

Wait.

Had she agreed to let him take her?

Not that she remembered.

But why look a gift horse in the mouth?

"That would be fine." Not as early as she'd planned to hit the road, but at least she was going.

"I'll see you then. We can stop for lunch on the way. This is going to be a great weekend."

As they rang off, Laura weighed her phone in her hand.

Too bad she didn't feel as confident about that as Nick sounded. Truth be told, being in his presence for four days was more apt to be nerve-racking and unsettling than relaxing.

But as long as they stayed around the family she should be safe.

Yet much as she wanted to protect her heart, she couldn't stop the tingle of anticipation that raced through her at the thought of Nick being part of her weekend.

Nor could she crush the little surge of foolish hope that maybe, despite the crowd that would gather at Mom's, he might find another opportunity to touch her hair again.

7

As he pulled up in front of her apartment the next morning at precisely ten o'clock, Nick let out the breath he hadn't even realized he was holding.

Laura was waiting out front for him.

Good news.

As skittish as she was around him, he'd half expected her to bail.

However…may as well face facts. The reason she hadn't was more a testament to her desire to see her family than to spend time with him.

Yes, she was attracted to him. Her eyes had spoken volumes both times he'd touched her. But she was running scared, thanks to demons in her past she hadn't yet revealed.

Perhaps this weekend, back on her home turf where she felt safe and secure, she might give him a clue what those demons were so he could figure out a way to help her overcome them.

For both their sakes.

Because the more he saw her, the more he wanted to see her. And the more he began to think there could be serious potential if he ever got past her barriers.

Before he even set the brake, she picked up her overnight bag and hurried down the walkway. By the time he slid from behind the wheel, she was waiting at the trunk.

“Good morning. I assume you want my bag in there.” She waved a hand toward the back of the car.

“That was the plan.” He popped the trunk, took her bag from her, and set it beside his duffel. “Were you waiting long?”

“No. I came out a couple of minutes ago. I knew you’d be on time. You’re a reliable guy.” She flashed him a smile

There were other words he’d prefer she apply to him, but on the bright side reliable was a positive quality.

“Let me get your door.” He circled around to the passenger side and opened it.

“Thanks.” She sidled past him and slid onto the seat, the fresh scent from her hair tantalizing his nose.

After she was in, he closed the door and retook his place behind the wheel. “Do you want to give me an address so my phone can guide me, or would you like to navigate?”

“I can direct you. It’s I-55 south most of the way.”

“Works for me.”

As he wound through the city streets toward the highway entrance, he gave her a surreptitious scan.

Her hands were clasped in her lap, her posture was rigid, and faint furrows dented her brow.

Man.

She was one big cluster of tension.

If he didn’t diffuse her anxiety it was going to be a very long ride.

“I had an interesting meeting with George Thompson this week.” Maybe talking about an impersonal subject like the arts center would calm her down.

“What about?”

“A few modifications I’d proposed now that construction is underway, which the board signed off on. They were also pleased we're on schedule. Keep that timetable in mind for your own planning purposes."

"Noted. It will be amazing to see my landscape design come to life. But just winning the project has given the company a huge boost. More and more jobs are rolling in. I owe you for that."

"No. You owe George. I got pulled in kicking and screaming. Not that I'm sorry in hindsight, but I wasn't enthusiastic at the beginning, as you know."

"Yes—and I don't blame you. My firm was an unknown quantity, and those can be disruptive. Not to mention scary." She peeked over at him. Cleared her throat. When she continued, there was a hint of…regret?...in her voice. "I need to tell you something."

Her tone didn't give him a warm and fuzzy feeling. But she was in the car and committed to this trip, so if she had something negative to say he'd have four days to try to counter it.

"Okay." He braced, tightening his grip on the wheel.

"I'm feeling kind of guilty about this weekend. I don't want to mislead you."

"About what?" As if he couldn't guess.

"My interest in a…personal…relationship."

Not a subject he'd planned to tackle less than an hour into their weekend, but maybe it wasn't a bad idea to put it on the table. Ignoring the elephant in the room wasn't going to make it go away.

"May I be honest?" At this point, it might be best to be candid—as diplomatically as possible.

She studied him for a moment, eyes uncertain. "I guess so."

"I've dated a lot of women. I'm not always the most clued-in guy, but I think I've learned to read signals—both deliberate and subliminal. And unless my instincts are failing, you're as interested in me as I am in you. I can see it in your eyes, your body language, your tone of voice. But I'm a patient man. I can wait, as long as you're willing to give us a chance."

She took a deep breath. "That was direct."

"I value honesty in a relationship. I think you do too. Otherwise you wouldn't have told me you were scared that night in the parking lot a couple of weeks ago."

"I still am. Maybe more than ever."

"Why?"

"Because I like you a lot. And if I'm not careful, I could get carried away—and maybe get hurt."

"Not by me." But *someone* had hurt her, and she obviously didn't trust her judgment about men. "And I'm fine with you setting the pace in this relationship."

"I appreciate that. But you may be wasting your time. I can't make any promises about the outcome."

"I'm not asking you to. I'm willing to take my chances. Fair enough?"

"For me, yes. I'm not sure it is for you."

"If I'm not worried about that, you shouldn't be either. Here's my suggestion. Let's put all the heavy stuff aside for the holiday and just enjoy our getaway. How does that sound?"

The tension in her features eased. "Good."

Keeping that goal in mind, Nick focused on lighter topics as they headed south, through rolling, wooded hills and farmland. And the farther away they got from the city, the more Laura seemed to relax.

So if all went well, perhaps by the time they returned to St. Louis she'd be more willing to give him a chance to prove he was a man she could trust not only on a date, but with the traumatic secrets she'd locked in her heart that kept her from taking a chance on love.

* * *

"Are you hungry?"

At Nick's question an hour into the drive, Laura nodded. "Yes." The case of nerves that had ruined her appetite for breakfast this morning had vanished, and there was a definite hollow in the pit of her stomach.

"I've been keeping an eye out, but our choices seem limited to the usual interstate fast-food places. Any preferences?"

She pursed her lips.

They weren't far from Becca's tea room—if Nick didn't mind a short detour.

"There's a place down this way I've been wanting to try, but it's a little off our path."

"Are we expected at any certain time?"

"No."

"Then let's give your place a shot. Where is it?"

"A few miles off the interstate, in Ste. Genevieve."

"Ah. The old French settlement. I've never been there."

"It's a charming town. A childhood friend of mine has a restaurant there, and a visit has been on my wish list. But I never seem to have any spare hours to drive down here. I follow her Facebook page, and the place has gotten excellent reviews."

"It sounds like a definite step up from fast food. You want to call up the directions on your phone?"

She did so, and within fifteen minutes they were parking in front of the restaurant, which was in the heart of the historic district.

Laura gave the charming country French decor a scan as they were led to their table by a white-haired woman with a pleasant round face. "Is Rebecca here today?"

The woman's eyes began to twinkle. "Rebecca is *always* here. Would you like me to ask her to come out?"

"If she has a minute, I'd appreciate that. Tell her it's Laura Taylor."

"This is an impressive menu." Nick perused the offerings as the hostess retreated. "Very imaginative and upscale. Not what you'd expect to find in a small town."

"Becca studied at the Culinary Institute of America and did internships with a couple of Michelin restaurants." Laura debated over her own selection before finally settling on croque monsieur.

As they finished placing their orders, her friend appeared in the doorway to the kitchen—looking gorgeous as always, her classic high cheekbones accentuated by the elegant French twist of her russet-colored hair. No wonder she'd been the envy of every girl in high school.

When their gazes met, Becca smiled and walked toward them.

Nick rose as she approached, and Laura stood as well.

"It's so good to see you, Laura." Becca gave her a hug.

"Likewise. I've been meaning to come down, but trying to get my business established requires more hours than there are in a day."

"Tell me about it." Becca rolled her eyes, then nodded toward Nick. "Do I get to meet your friend?"

"Of course." Laura did the introductions, then gave Nick an aside. "Becca is her childhood nickname. Family and close friends from those days still use it, but in the real world she goes by Rebecca."

"You can call me either, though." She smiled at Nick. "If you're a friend of Laura's, you're a friend of mine. May I join you for a minute?"

"Please." Nick retrieved a chair from an empty table nearby.

"So what brings you to Ste. Genevieve?" Becca gave the busy restaurant a practiced sweep before refocusing on them.

"We're on our way to the Anderson Fourth of July reunion." Laura draped her napkin over her lap.

"Of course. I should have remembered. Those gatherings are legendary. You must rate to be invited." She gave Nick a once-over.

He responded with an engaging grin. "In the interest of full disclosure, I invited myself."

"Actually, he came to my rescue." Laura filled Becca in on the truck saga. "So how is it going here? You've gotten some great press in St. Louis."

"No complaints, and the publicity has definitely helped. But it's a lot of hard work, and the long hours don't leave much time for anything else. Still, it's gratifying to see the business grow. Brad tells me you're doing well too."

"Brad's her brother—and my minister." Laura passed that on to Nick before responding to Becca. "No complaints on my end either. Hard work really does pay."

"But remember that old saying about all work and no play." One side of Nick's mouth quirked up. "Laura is a hard sell on that concept, though."

"She's been a workaholic since we were kids." Becca arched an eyebrow at her.

"It takes one to know one." Laura returned her look.

Becca gave a soft laugh and lifted her palms. "What can I say?"

"I'm sorry to interrupt." The hostess paused at their table, giving them all an apologetic sweep. "But the repairman is here, Rebecca."

"Thanks, Rose. Tell him I'll be there in a minute." As the woman bustled off, Becca turned back to the two of them. "Sorry to run, although I suspect three's a crowd anyway. Laura, it was wonderful to see you. Please stop by again soon. And Nick, we do very romantic dinners here on Friday and Saturday nights."

He hitched up one side of his mouth as heat crept across Laura's cheeks. "I'll keep that in mind."

Laura was saved from having to respond by the arrival of their food, and Nick didn't venture into personal territory during the remainder of their meal, other than asking her about her hometown.

By the time a delicious and decadently rich chocolate torte arrived, compliments of the house, she was starting to relax again.

Conversation flowed easily during the remainder of the trip, and only as they approached their destination did Nick segue to the holiday plans. "Why don't you brief me on the agenda and cast of characters?"

"There isn't much of an agenda. Today and tomorrow will be low-key. Church in the morning and dinner at Aunt Gladys's tomorrow are the only planned activities, but there will be lots of impromptu visiting. On the Fourth, Mom has everyone over for a cookout. Then we play horseshoes or croquet and shoot off fireworks in the field after dark. Tuesday we can head back whenever we want. You can bow out of any activities that don't interest you."

"I'm in for everything."

Hmm.

If he was a churchgoing man, that was a plus.

"As for the cast, I'll stick with the main players." She ticked them off on her fingers. "There's my brother, John, and his family, who live in town. My brother, Dennis, who lives in Memphis, will be up for the weekend and staying at the house. Aunt Gladys and Uncle George have five kids, most of whom are married, and a lot of them will come back for the Fourth. A bunch of other relatives will show up too, but I'll introduce them as needed."

He glanced over at her. "You didn't mention your dad."

"No." She swallowed past the pressure in her throat. "He died eleven years ago. I was the only girl in the family, and he and I shared a special bond. I still miss him every day."

"I'm sorry."

"Me too. He died right after Fourth of July—one of the few I didn't spend with the family." Regret weighed down her words.

"How come? I got the impression this was a sacred ritual."

"It is now. But I missed several years when I was married." And that was all she was going to say about that. "We're getting close to the house. You'll be turning right about a mile up the road."

Thankfully he followed her lead and let the subject of the missed Fourth of July visits drop.

And if he continued to be that tuned in to her boundary-setting cues for the remainder of the trip, maybe she could relax and enjoy this much-needed break.

* * *

As Nick turned into the gravel driveway that led to a modest white frame house on the outskirts of town, the front screen door opened and an older, slightly stout woman in a faded apron appeared.

Laura leaned forward, lips bowing. "Mom's been watching for us."

Even before he set the brake, Laura was out of the car and jogging toward her mother, who hurried down the steps and pulled her into a tight hug.

"Oh, honey, it's so good to see you." Her words carried in the quiet air as he got out of the car.

"It's good to be home, Mom."

He remained by the car until Laura's mother stepped back and smiled at him. "You must be Nick."

"Guilty."

She crossed to him and held out her hand. "Welcome." She gave his fingers a firm squeeze, then spoke over her shoulder to Laura. "You didn't tell me your young man was so handsome, honey."

Crimson spots bloomed on Laura's cheeks. "He's not my young man, Mom. Like I told you last night on the phone, we're business associates and friends."

"So you did." But the twinkle in her mother's eyes suggested she wasn't buying that.

Good to know he wasn't the only one who'd concluded Laura was more interested than she was letting on.

"It's a pleasure to meet you, Mrs. Anderson. And thank you for inviting me. It was very generous of you."

"Not at all. We're glad to have you. And please call me Evelyn. Now let's go in and get you both settled. Laura, could you take Nick up to John's old room? I've got a pie in the oven that's just about done."

"Sure."

"Take your time unpacking. I didn't know when everyone would be arriving so I just made a big pot of chili. It'll be there whenever you're hungry."

Nick circled around to the back of his car, Laura on his

heels. As soon as he opened the trunk she reached for her bag, but he beat her to it. "I've got it." He settled the strap of the overnight case on his shoulder.

"You don't have to carry my luggage."

"Both of us packed light." He pulled out his duffel and closed the trunk. "I can manage two bags. Why don't you lead the way and clear the path?"

She hesitated for a moment, then walked ahead and opened the screen door for him. "Your room is up the stairs, first door on the right."

After edging past her, he entered, ascended the steps, and nudged open the first door with his shoulder. Set his bag inside the door as he gave the space a scan.

A double bed, oak chest, and desk with chair sat on a braided rug that covered the polished plank floors, and woven curtains hung at the window. The room was simple, spotless, and compact.

It was also hot.

Really hot.

Beads of perspiration popped out on his forehead, and he gave them a discreet swipe before pivoting back to Laura.

Her brow rumpled as she regarded him. "I should have warned you that Mom doesn't have central air. Just a couple of room units."

"It wouldn't have made me change my mind about coming."

"Are you sure? I mean, I grew up like this, so I'm used to it. But most people live in air conditioning today. Especially in Missouri in July."

That was true.

But he'd survive.

"I'm sure the ceiling fan will help." He waved toward the motionless blades.

"It will. The house cools off a lot at night anyway, and we don't spend much time up here during the day. But I should have told you."

"Hey." He touched her arm. "I'll be fine. Now, where do you want this?" He tapped her overnight case.

"I'm right next door."

He followed her down the hall and into a pale blue room rimmed with a delicate floral wallpaper border and filled with white wicker furniture.

"You can put it there." Laura motioned toward a chair in one corner.

After setting her bag down, he turned his attention to a Monet print of waterlilies featuring a bridge over a pond. "Nice."

"Thanks. It was a high-school graduation gift from Mom and Dad. I love Monet. All the Impressionists, actually."

He leaned closer to study it. "This is a high-quality print." He straightened up and turned back to her. "I'm surprised you didn't take it with you when you moved away."

Some emotion he couldn't identify flickered in her eyes. "My husband wasn't a fan of Impressionism. I may take it to my apartment one day."

Her husband didn't like Impressionism, so she wasn't comfortable putting up a print that was a gift from her parents?

An alert began to beep in his mind.

All along, he'd assumed she was a grieving widow. But was there more to that story?

Based on the set of her jaw, however, he wasn't going to hear any details today. "I'm going to freshen up. Why don't I meet you downstairs in about fifteen minutes?"

"Sounds like a plan."

He returned to his room and wandered over to the window. Stared out over the distant fields.

The barriers Laura had erected were formidable, and pushing wasn't going to break them down. In fact, it would no doubt do the opposite.

So he'd have to bide his time, prove to her he was trustworthy, and hope that down the road she'd crack a door to her heart and let him in.

Because if she didn't, this relationship was going nowhere.

And that was a depressing thought on what was supposed to be a festive holiday weekend.

* * *

Maybe it would have been wiser to forego this trip to see her family.

As Laura splashed cold water on her face in the steamy bathroom, she tried to tamp down her apprehension.

She should have realized that here, on her home turf, among her family, Nick would learn more about her than she was ready to share.

But at this point all she could do was run interference.

She opened the bathroom door. Peeked out.

Nick's door was still closed.

Good.

She could use a few minutes alone with the family.

After descending the stairs as quietly as she could, wincing with every creak, she headed to the bright, sunny kitchen.

John was sitting at the polished oak table trying with zero success to convince eight-month-old Daniel to eat a spoonful of strained peas, while Dana cleared the remainder of three-year-old Susan's meal off the table.

"Aunt Laura!" Susan catapulted herself across the room.

Laura bent down to catch her, sweeping her up with a smile. "My goodness, what a big girl you are now."

After tolerating the hug for a few seconds, Susan squirmed to be set loose.

As Laura set her niece down, John gave her a harried smile. "Hi, Sis. We'll clear out of here in a minute so you can enjoy your late lunch or early dinner in peace."

"Don't rush on my account." Laura sat, rested an elbow on the table, and cupped her chin in her palm as Daniel spit out his latest bite of peas. "This is entertaining."

"You wouldn't want to take over, would you? Have some bonding time with your nephew?" John gave her a hopeful look.

"Nope." She angled toward her sister-in-law. "Are you keeping my brother in line with division of child-care duties?"

Dana's lips twitched. "It can be a challenge. Especially when it comes to diapering."

"I'll bet."

"Hey." John gave his wife an indignant look. "I do my share."

Dana dropped a kiss on his head as she passed by. "Sometimes under duress—but yes, you do."

"See? I shoulder my share of the pea-spitting." He wiped another green glob off the table.

"Kudos to you." Laura gave him a mock salute.

As Dana followed Susan into the next room, John smiled across the table. "It's good to see you, Sis."

"It's good to be home." She reached over and squeezed his free hand. "Is Dennis here yet?"

The screen door banged. "Anybody here?"

John grinned. "Speak of the devil." He raised his volume. "We're in the kitchen."

Footsteps pounded down the hall, and a few moments later Dennis appeared on the threshold. "Who owns the sporty red number out front? Man, what a set of wheels."

"Hello to you too." Laura arched an eyebrow at him.

"Oh. Sorry." He crossed the room and bent down to give her a squeeze. "Hi. So who owns the car?"

"The guy she brought down for the weekend." John continued trying to coax Daniel to eat.

Dennis blinked. Lasered in on her "You brought a guy down here? Where is he?"

Folding her arms, Laura scowled at her brothers. "You've got it backward. *He* brought *me.* My truck gave out, and he offered to drive me down. It was a nice gesture from a friend. Period. Don't try to read any more into it."

Dennis snorted. "Give me a break. No guy with a car like that drives three hours to stay in an unairconditioned house in a town small enough to spit across just because he's nice."

The lack of air conditioning had nothing to do with the heat that spread across her cheeks. "I knew this was a mistake. I should have just stayed home."

"Hey. You two leave your sister alone." Dana reentered, Susan on her hip. "If she says this man is just a friend, then that's all he is."

The screen door to the back porch opened, and Mom bustled in. "Oh, Laura. I didn't hear you come down. Are you and your young man ready for some chili?"

As her two brothers smirked at her, she crossed her arms on the table and buried her face in them. "I give up."

Everyone started asking questions at once, and Laura ignored them all—until there was a sudden hush.

Great.

Nick must have shown up.

Slowly she raised her head.

His gaze met hers, more curious than uncomfortable despite the attention being focused on him.

Laura cleared her throat and shot a warning glance at her family. "Nick, meet my brothers John and Dennis, and John's wife, Dana. Also my niece and nephew, Susan and Daniel. Daniel's the one with the green slime running down his chin that's dripping onto John's shirt."

John muttered something unintelligible as he grabbed a napkin and wiped at the stain.

"Nice to meet you." Dennis stuck out his hand. "Great car."

"Thanks."

"I'd shake hands, but to spare you pea slime, I'll just say hello." John grinned at him.

"Nice to meet you." Nick's mouth flexed. "And I appreciate your consideration."

"Let's leave these two in peace to enjoy their food, John." Dana set Susan down and swung Daniel onto her hip. "Nick, it's a pleasure. I'm sure we'll see a lot of you this weekend."

"I'll look forward to it."

"We'll be back later, Mom." John gave her a peck on the cheek.

"Good. Drive safe. Dennis, have some chili."

"Don't mind if I do." He helped himself, then turned a chair backward at the table and straddled it.

"Nick, go ahead and find a seat." Her mother put bowls and utensils on the table.

As the two men joined her, Laura filled a bowl with chili.

Fortunately, Dennis's boisterous chatter kept Nick occupied while they ate, giving her a chance to think.

Her family's reaction to Nick's presence wasn't really surprising. After all, he was the first man she'd brought home since Joe's death. In truth, she'd never brought *anyone* home except Joe. Nick being here was bound to cause a stir.

"This is great chili, Evelyn." Her chauffeur continued to chow down. "Does Laura have the recipe?"

"Yes. She's an excellent cook when she has the time."

"I know." He smiled at her, his warm look doing nothing to dispel her claim that he was only here because he'd provided her with a ride for her weekend getaway.

Laura swallowed a mouthful of chili. Washed it down with a long drink of water.

If this kept up, it was going to be a *very* long weekend.

One she could quickly come to regret.

8

From his shady spot under a tree on Sunday afternoon, Nick watched Laura help her mother and aunt clear away the remains of the fried chicken Gladys had prepared for more than thirty relatives.

Thankfully his offer of assistance had been turned down, freeing him to seek relief from the heat under the spreading branches of this oak. Nor was he alone. Other than a few more energetic members of the group, who were engaged in a spirited game of horseshoes, everyone else seemed content to do nothing more strenuous than shoo away an occasional fly.

And it was a perfect chance to watch Laura unobserved.

From a distance, she could pass for a teenager in her shorts and T-shirt. Even up close she seemed younger. The lines of tension around her mouth and eyes had vanished, and her occasional carefree laugh gave him a glimpse of the woman she'd been before some demon from her past tamped down her joy.

But she was doing her best to make sure the two of them weren't alone.

That was a problem.

Because any hope that she might open up a little in this more relaxed setting would come to naught if he couldn't find a way to spirit her away from the group.

"Land, it's a hot one." Gladys strolled over, fanning herself with a folded newspaper, followed by Laura and her mother. The two older women opened lawn chairs, while Laura dropped to the ground next to him. "Does anyone want iced tea or lemonade? Nick?"

"No, thank you. I'm still too full from your amazing dinner to put one more thing in my stomach."

"I'm glad you liked it." Gladys exchanged a glance with Evelyn before focusing on her niece. "Laura, why don't you show Nick the spring? It's much cooler down there."

Laura jerked her attention away from the game of horseshoes, a hint of panic blooming in her eyes.

"Um…it's a long walk, Aunt Gladys. I doubt anyone wants to go hiking in this weather."

"It's not that far. If I were as young as you two, I'd head there myself."

"A cool spring sounds appealing." He plucked a blade of grass. Twirled it between his fingers. "I'm game."

"There you go, Laura." Evelyn backed up her sister.

When Laura didn't budge, Nick pushed himself to his feet and held out his hand. "I'm all for finding a cooler spot, even if it takes a little effort to get there. Will you show me the way?"

After a brief hesitation, she put her hand in his and he drew her to her feet. But she eased it free as soon as she was standing.

"We'll be back soon." She sent her mother and aunt an irked look.

"Take your time." Her mother waved off the comment, either oblivious to the undertones or ignoring them. "You won't miss anything here."

Laura turned to him. "It's down the road and through the woods." She waved a hand in a northerly direction.

"If we're not back by dark, send out a search party." Nick

grinned at his two allies. "Or not."

Evelyn laughed. "I'm sure you'll take good care of her. Have fun."

Laura struck off for the road, leaving him to follow in her wake.

"Hey! What's the rush?" He broke into a jog to catch up with her.

"I thought you wanted to see the spring."

"I do. But it's not going anywhere, is it?"

She huffed out a breath and slowed her gait. "No."

"That's what I like in a tour guide. Enthusiasm." Despite his teasing tone, her demeanor remained glum.

"Sorry. I just hate being railroaded into anything."

At her nuanced comment, he stopped.

"What's wrong?" She paused and looked back at him.

"If you'd rather not go, we can kill the idea." If she wasn't a willing partner in this outing it was doomed to fail anyway.

She studied him, indecision flaring in her eyes. But in the end, she capitulated. "No. Let's go. It *is* cooler there, and I expect you could use a break from all the family togetherness."

The taut muscles in his shoulders relaxed. "I like your family, but I wouldn't be averse to a little quiet time."

"It's definitely quiet at the spring."

After walking in silence for several minutes under the relentless heat of the late-afternoon sun, Laura shot him a rueful glance. "Are you regretting this outing yet?"

"Depends on how much farther it is." He swiped the back of his hand across his forehead.

"We're coming up on the path." She pointed to a curve in the road about a hundred yards ahead. "It cuts through the woods, so we'll be in the shade for the duration. The spring's about a ten-minute walk from the road."

"I can handle that."

Once they turned onto the path, he paused and pulled out his handkerchief. Mopped his brow. The leafy canopy provided a modicum of relief from the heat, but not enough to cool him down.

"I told you it was too hot to hike." She propped her hands on her hips.

"I'm not complaining." But he couldn't even remember when he'd last been this hot. Except maybe the time he and a college buddy had hiked to the bottom of the Grand Canyon in August. Not one of their smartest adventures.

He followed her down the narrow path, and within fifteen minutes they were sitting side-by-side on a large rock, their feet immersed in a stream that was fed by the bubbling spring a few yards away.

Bliss.

"This is a great spot." He leaned back on the palms of his hands.

"Yes, it is. I came here often when I was a kid. This area was a wonderful place to grow up—fresh air, open spaces, pastures to run in, trees to climb, apples to pick."

"Sounds idyllic."

She lifted a foot. Watched the water drip back into the stream. "It was, in a lot of ways. We didn't have much in terms of worldly wealth, but we were rich in all the ways that mattered—family, faith, and plenty of love. You may have picked that up this weekend."

"In spades."

"It's such a blessing to grow up in a close family. That's a priceless legacy."

"I hear you. I grew up in a family like that too. But not everyone is so lucky."

She drew up her legs and wrapped her arms around them, resting her chin on her knees. "I know. That's one of the reasons I got involved with Christian Youth Outreach. Those poor kids have no idea what it's like to live in a warm, caring, supportive atmosphere. Outreach can't make up for that lapse, but it does provide programs that help instill solid values and give kids a sense of self-worth.

The dappled sunlight played across her face, highlighting the faint shadows under her eyes that were clear evidence she worked too hard. Yet she still found time to give to others.

What an amazing woman.

"The world could use more people like you."

At his quiet comment, she shook her head. "A lot of people do way more than me." Then she filled her lungs and switched back to the previous topic. "This spot brings back so many good memories."

"It must have been hard to leave here."

"In some ways, yes. But I was very much in love." She leaned down. Trailed her fingers through the cool water. "Besides, I had visions of re-creating this lifestyle in St. Louis. I assumed there would be an area with a small-town feel, and I found it in Webster Groves. When I was first married I used to love to drive through there and admire the old Victorian houses with the big yards. I always hoped someday we'd have one."

Instead, she lived in a four-family flat in the heart of the city with a tiny patch of grass for a yard.

Because her husband had died before they could make her dream come true? Or had he not shared her love of Victorians, much as he hadn't shared her love of Impressionist paintings?

Maybe if he kept her talking she'd give him a few clues.

"What sort of Victorian did you have in mind?"

Her expression grew wistful as she watched the water tumble over the rocks. "One with a big porch on three sides, with lots of gingerbread trim and cupolas, and fireplaces, and an arbor covered with morning glories that led to a rose garden. There would be ferns and rocking chairs on the porch, and in the backyard, a tire swing." The brightness in her demeanor dimmed. "But that wasn't in God's plan for me."

At the slight catch in her voice, he had to fight a powerful urge to take her hand. "I'm sorry you never got your house."

She shrugged and offered him a strained smile. "It is what it is. But I have to admit that sometimes I drive over there just to look at the houses and daydream."

"There's nothing wrong with dreaming."

Her features hardened. "There is when you have no way of making those dreams come true. If I've learned one thing in the past few years, it's to be realistic."

"So no more dreams?"

"Only ones I can control, where if you do certain things there's a predictable outcome. Like my business, for example."

"And *un*like relationships." The words tumbled out before he could rein then in.

Blast.

In a second or two she'd probably jump to her feet, shut down the conversation, and take off back through the woods.

But she didn't.

After a long moment, she looked over at him. "Yes."

Now that he was in for an inch, may as well go for a mile. "I know you're scared of being hurt, and that can be a powerful fear. But don't you ever get lonely?"

She brushed off a leaf from her shorts. "I have my family."

"That's not what I mean."

At least she didn't pretend to misunderstand. "I know. But I've learned to handle that kind of loneliness."

"I assume there's a very good reason you're so scared."

Her throat worked for a moment, and then she began pulling on her socks and shoes. "There is."

That was all she offered.

And that was all she was *going* to offer.

For today, anyway.

Stifling his disappointment, he reached for his own shoes and tugged them on in silence.

Once she finished tying her laces, Laura stood. "We ought to start back. We've been gone longer than I intended."

Nick rose too. "I'm not a bad listener, for a guy, if you ever want to talk about why you built that wall you hide behind."

She flushed and turned away. Started walking. "I don't believe in dwelling on the past."

"Then why are you letting it control your future?"

Her step faltered for a moment, but she quickly picked up her pace again. "I'm not."

"Are you sure about that?"

Instead of answering, she walked faster, putting more distance between them.

Nick blew out a breath.

Whatever happened to his plan to move slow and build trust?

Now he might have to start from scratch again.

He lengthened his stride to catch up with her, but as he drew close she suddenly stumbled. Pitched forward. Went down hard.

Pulse lurching, he broke into a jog and dropped down beside

her. "Are you all right?"

She sucked in a breath. "Yes. I'm fine." She pushed herself into a sitting position and scanned the ground. "There's the culprit." She pointed to an exposed tree root. "If I'd been paying more attention, I wouldn't have fallen. I know better than to barrel ahead. That's how people get hurt." Her voice was shaky, but the resolve in her eyes wasn't. Suggesting there was a deeper meaning to her comment that didn't necessarily bode well for their relationship.

Stifling that unsettling thought, he stood and held out his hand. "Let me help you up."

"Thanks." She took it, and as he pulled her to her feet a long scrape on the side of her other arm caught his eye.

He frowned as it began to bleed. "You've got a nasty cut on your arm."

After giving it a cursory glance, she shrugged. "I think I grazed the tree trunk as I fell. It's not deep. I'll deal with it when we get back."

"I'd be glad to help. It's in kind of a hard spot to reach."

Her gaze locked with his, and a quiver rippled through her. "Thank you, but I can m-manage. I'm used to being on my own."

Any second now, she was going to pull her hand free from his.

But she didn't.

"It's okay to let people help. Especially people who care about you."

Her breath hitched, and a surge of longing flooded her eyes.

He gritted his teeth.

Did she have any idea what a powerful message she was sending?

She moistened her lips, and his gaze flicked to them.

His shaky self-control splintered.

Without making a conscious decision, he eased closer to her.

She didn't back away.

Did that mean she might be receptive to a brief, gentle, exploratory kiss?

Her eyes said yes.

So did her slight sway toward him.

Slowly, he leaned down. If she gave any indication his kiss was unwelcome, he'd back off in a heartbeat. But when a desirable woman sent such strong signals—even if they were subliminal—a man could only resist for so long.

The warmth of her breath caressed his lips as he angled his head and came within a whisper of—

At a sudden sound of crashing brush behind him, Laura gasped. Jerked back.

Biting back a word he never said, Nick straightened up and swiveled around.

A doe and fawn stood motionless a few yards away, ears twitching. After a few moments, they bolted into the woods and disappeared.

Nick took a long, steadying breath.

He'd been close. So close to tasting her lips.

But maybe this was for the best. Laura could have been as spooked as those deer if he'd followed through, no matter the invitation she'd been sending. She might have bolted, as they had.

As for her reaction in the aftermath?

Who knew?

Best to play this by ear.

He swallowed. Turned.

Laura had retreated a few feet, and her arms were wrapped around her middle.

She was back to running scared.

But how could they ignore what had almost happened?

He leaned a shoulder against an adjacent tree and shoved his fingers into his pocket. "Those deer didn't have the best timing."

Her throat worked. "Depends on your perspective, I guess."

"What's yours?"

"Their appearance was well-timed. I'm not ready for what was about to happen."

"Based on the signals I was picking up, you're readier than you think you are."

She brushed back a few wisps of hair that had escaped her ponytail, the tremor in her fingers impossible to miss. "You sound like Sam."

"You have a wise best friend."

"About some things. But it's dangerous to give your emotions the upper hand."

"I don't disagree in general. However, it's okay to do that if you're with someone you can trust."

She exhaled. "Trust doesn't come easy for me."

"Understood." He called up a smile and pushed off from the tree. "But I'm going to work hard to earn it. You ready to head back?"

"Yes."

He let her precede him on the narrow path, falling in beside her again once they reached the road. But despite his attempt to initiate a conversation, she was mostly quiet during the remainder of their walk.

And for the rest of the evening and the next morning she

doubled down on her evasive maneuvers, doing her best to ensure they didn't have any time alone together.

Translation?

She didn't want a repeat of that moment in the woods, and was scared that it could happen again if they were alone together.

Which suggested her feelings ran as strong as his, and that she wasn't immune to the electricity sparking between them.

That was encouraging.

What *wasn't* encouraging was how she left him high and dry during the Fourth of July spread at her Mom's.

By the time he filled his plate and made his way toward the long tables set up in the yard, she'd already found a seat between her niece and her brother.

Blast.

Nice as her family was, he'd planned to sit next to her for the holiday meal.

"Susan, where's your fork?" John leaned around Laura, his voice carrying across the yard.

"Gone." She pointed under the table.

"I'll get her another one." Laura stood.

"Thanks, Sis."

As she headed for the buffet table, Nick crossed to John. "Do you think you could squeeze one more in here?"

Her brother grinned. "No problem."

When Laura returned, a plastic fork in hand, she stopped a few feet away and narrowed her eyes at her brother.

"Nick was looking for a seat, and we had plenty of room here." He scooted over, and Nick did likewise, leaving space for her to join them.

"I don't want to crowd you." She gave Susan the fork and reached for her plate. "I'll go sit with Mom."

"Mom's table is full." John waved a hand across the lawn.

"Will you join us if I promise not to nibble on anything except my ear of corn?" Nick waggled his eyebrows at her.

As amused glances were directed their way, Laura capitulated. But she ate fast and skipped dessert, opting to join a game of croquet.

As Nick watched her walk away, John spoke. "She's a slow mover."

He turned his attention to the other man. "I've noticed. Is she like that with all men?"

"As far as I know, Joe was the only man in her life. If there was anyone else after he died, she's never mentioned him. Laura's always been closemouthed about her private affairs."

"So I've discovered."

"Hang in. You're making progress."

"No much that I can see."

"She let you drive her down here. That's huge."

"She was desperate."

"That's not the only reason. She wouldn't share her family with someone she didn't care about."

"Thanks for the pep talk."

Hours later, after everyone had turned in for the night, he crossed to the window in his room and opened it as high as he could.

While the weekend hadn't gone exactly as he'd hoped, he *had* learned a lot about Laura's roots and her family. And if John's take was right, there was hope for him with her.

He leaned closer to the window. Tried in vain to catch a breath of cooler air.

How could the heat still be oppressive at eleven o'clock? And the ceiling fan wasn't helping at all. Sleeping in this sauna would be impossible.

Maybe if he went outside for a few minutes, cooled off a little, it would be easier to fall asleep.

Nick crossed to the door. Eased it open.

The hall was dark, suggesting everyone else had found it easier to sleep than he had.

He made his way down the stairs, cut through the kitchen, and exited onto the back porch, holding the screen door so it wouldn't bang shut behind him.

It was definitely cooler out here.

Maybe he ought to grab his pillow and rack out on the—

"Hello, Nick."

He swung around.

Evelyn spoke again from the shadowed porch swing. "Sorry. I didn't mean to startle you."

"No worries. I thought everyone was in bed." He moved closer to her and leaned back against the porch railing, ankles crossed, palms flat on the smooth wood of the top rail behind him.

"Sometimes on hot nights I like to come down and swing for a while. Walter—Laura's father—and I used to do that, and I can't seem to break the habit."

"Laura speaks very warmly of him."

She nodded. "Those two had a great relationship. But the whole family is close. It was hard on all of us when Laura got married and moved to St. Louis. We figured they'd come to visit often, but it didn't work out that way."

As long as Evelyn had broached that subject, maybe she'd reveal a bit more with a few discreet prompts. "I'm surprised. I can see how much Laura loves being here with all of you."

"We were too." She continued to swing, using the toe of one

foot to keep the momentum going. "I expect it had something to do with Joe, even though she never said that."

"Wasn't he from this area too?"

"Yes. But he didn't have as much family here. And he had bigger dreams than our small town could offer." A nuance in her tone put him on alert.

"Is that a bad thing?"

"No. Dreams are fine. But Joe was one of those people who always seem to have their head in the clouds, building castles in the air and never putting the foundation under them. Laura's just the opposite. She plans everything to the nth degree and persists until she succeeds."

"I've definitely seen evidence of that." But he was more interested in her husband at the moment. "John mentioned today that Joe was the only guy she ever dated."

"That's true. And they were so young when they got married. Too young, in my opinion." She shook her head, tut-tutting. "But there was no convincing them of that. To be honest, I never thought they were the best match. Still, I was shocked when she left him. Laura isn't one to walk away from obligations or commitments."

Nick stared at Evelyn.

Laura had left her husband?

Why hadn't she told him that?

And what had caused her marriage to fall apart?

"Do you know why she left?" Maybe he was prying, but he couldn't not ask at this point.

"No. She never gave us much of an explanation other than to say there were problems. But I expect they were serious if she gave up."

So did he.

Yet what on earth could have happened?

Laura had said earlier this weekend that she'd been in love with Joe. Enough to leave her hometown and the family she cherished.

But somewhere along the way, that love had soured. And a failed marriage could make anyone nervous about embarking on a new relationship.

Her fear and caution, however, went beyond the normal bounds.

Evelyn held her watch toward the dim porch light. "My, it's getting late. I should get to bed." She stood. "Sleep well."

"You too."

He remained where he was as she disappeared inside, then turned toward the backyard. Filled his lungs with the night air as he gripped the railing.

Coming out here had cooled him off.

But after all the questions his chat with Evelyn had raised, there was no way he was going to sleep well tonight.

9

So much for coming back from her trip relaxed and refreshed. As the clock inched toward three in the morning on Wednesday, Laura threw back the covers.

She could blame her restlessness on the heat, but that wouldn't be fair.

This was all Nick's fault.

And hers, if she was honest.

In fact, it was mostly hers.

Staring at the dark ceiling, she blew out a breath.

She couldn't blame him for being subdued on the drive home yesterday. Not after she'd gone out of her way to keep him at arm's length during their trip. Not after sending mixed signals on their hike to the spring. Not after doing everything she could to discourage his interest.

Heck, he was probably regretting that he'd ever offered to take her home.

She punched her pillow and flopped onto her side.

No wonder he'd carried her bag upstairs in silence yesterday and made his escape as fast as possible. Even a man with the patience of Job would give up eventually.

But she ought to be glad he wasn't pushing. That's what she'd wanted.

Right?

Yet if that was true, why was there a hollow feeling in the pit of her stomach?

Quashing that question, she forced herself to take long, slow breaths, doing her best to empty her mind. If she didn't get some sleep, she'd be a zombie tomorrow.

Scratch that.

She'd be a zombie *today*.

At last, she drifted into a fitful slumber.

But five-thirty came much too fast.

By the time she was dressed, her foreman had arrived to take her to the office. Thankfully, he'd also agreed to drop her at the garage tonight so she could pick up her car.

"Morning, Ken." She took a long gulp of coffee from her insulated mug as she slid into the passenger seat of his car. "Thanks again for picking me up."

"Happy to do it. Car trouble stinks." He squinted at her. "You look tired."

"That's what happens when you only log two and a half hours' sleep."

"Did you get back late from your trip?"

"No. Just couldn't sleep." She set her laptop case by her feet. "Let's stop by the job sites first. How did everything go yesterday?"

Ken filled her in as they drove to the two sites, then dropped her at the office. "I'll be back about four, if that's okay."

"Whenever is fine. I have plenty of paperwork to keep me busy. But I have to admit it will feel odd to spend a whole day at my desk."

He grinned. "Yeah. The crews won't know what to think."

"Well, I'll be popping back onto the sites tomorrow throughout the day."

As Ken drove away, she dug out the key for her office. Thank goodness she'd found someone so solid and reliable to fill the foreman role. It had been hard to let go of that hands-on role, but with the volume of work she was juggling now there'd been no option. Between paperwork and new design projects, she was slammed. All thanks to the arts center commission.

Best of all, the business had finally turned a corner and a more profitable road lay ahead. One that might even make her more comfortable splurging on air conditioning at night.

For the remainder of the day she was heads-down on design work, except for one client meeting. But when it got close to four she paused long enough to call the garage.

As soon as Dave greeted her, he gave her the bad news straight up. "I was just getting ready to call you. I'm afraid the part hasn't come in yet. I kept thinking it might show up this afternoon, but it didn't. I'm sorry."

Laura pinched the bridge of her nose. "It's not your fault. Do you think it will be here tomorrow?"

"Absolutely. I don't know what held it up today. I expect it'll come first thing in the morning. I'll call you as soon as your truck's ready."

"Okay. Thanks." Heaving a sigh, she ended the call.

Her planned stops at the grocery store and laundromat would have to wait until tomorrow.

Leaving her with way too much downtime to brood about Nick in her empty—and lonely—apartment.

May as well stay here for a while and catch a bus home later. Besides, her office could use a bit of straightening up, and she was usually too busy during the day to tackle decluttering.

After texting Ken about the change in plans, securing another lift from him tomorrow, and tidying up her workspace, she hunkered back down over a set of landscape plans for a new restaurant with patio seating.

In the end, hunger pangs forced her to call it a day. Besides, it was already seven-thirty and her eyelids were drooping after her restless night.

On the plus side, she shouldn't have any trouble dozing off tonight.

Laura picked up her cell. Weighed it in her hand.

No call from Nick today—not that she'd expected one, after his fast exit last night when he dropped her off.

He'd probably written her off for good.

And if he had, she had no one to blame but herself.

Shoulders drooping, she picked up her purse. No reason to take her laptop home tonight, since she'd be back in the morning.

After locking the door, she made her way to the bus stop. An uber would be more convenient, but the bus was much cheaper. And old frugality habits died hard.

The wait at the bus stop was lengthy, and by the time she boarded and was on her way dusk was descending.

Hmm.

Maybe she should have checked the schedule. It had been a while since she'd taken a bus, and it seemed they ran much less often in the evening than she remembered.

A conclusion borne out at the next stop, where she waited about twice as long as she expected for her connection.

By the time she finally disembarked two blocks from her apartment, night had fallen and utter weariness had set in.

As the bus disappeared in a cloud of noxious fumes, she wrinkled her nose and trudged toward her apartment.

Once off the bus route, Laura slowed her pace on the dim

side street, picking her way carefully down the sidewalk as she dodged cracks. It would help if the headlights from passing cars provided a bit of illumination, but these small streets didn't see much traffic.

Despite the lingering midday heat, and despite her assurance to Nick that the area was safe, a shiver rippled through her.

It wasn't the best part of town, after all.

Maybe she should reach deep for what little energy she had in reserve and pick up her pace. It wouldn't hurt to have her pepper gel in hand, either.

As she hurried down the street, she dug through her purse. Came up empty.

Oh, right.

The canister had expired, and she'd set it on the kitchen counter to remind herself to replace it.

A chore she hadn't yet gotten around to.

Oh, well.

She was almost home.

But a block from her apartment, a strange prickling at the back of her neck jacked up her pulse.

Step faltering, she turned. Scanned the sidewalk behind her.

Nothing but shadows.

She started forward again. There was no reason for this sudden case of jitters. It must have been brought on by the power of suggestion and intensified by her weariness.

Nevertheless, she lengthened her stride, hugging her shoulder bag close to her side.

When she at last turned the corner and her apartment came into view, she exhaled. As soon as she passed the last patch of darkness up ahead, she'd be home—and safe.

But the instant she entered that murky stretch, a figure

lunged at her. Hands grabbed her purse, trying to jerk it away from her shoulder.

No!

She tightened her grip and spun toward the mugger. It was a man, tall and broad-shouldered, his features shadowed beneath the brim of a baseball cap pulled low over his eyes,

The freeze-frame of shock at her resistance lasted only a second on his part before he sprang toward her again.

Adrenaline spiking, she responded with a kick to his groin—a self-defense move she'd learned long ago.

His grunt told her she'd hit pay dirt.

As he doubled over, she delivered an upward strike to his nose with the heel of her palm.

Then she snatched the purse strap out of his hands and began to run, praying her aggressive response would discourage him.

Unfortunately, it didn't.

After a string of obscenities burned her ears, footsteps pounded behind her.

Seconds later the man grabbed her arm and jerked her around.

Before she could scream, a fist slammed into her face.

Her head snapped back, bright pinpoints of light filling her field of vision. She staggered. Fell. Blood began flowing from her nose, and one eye started to water, blurring her vision.

Nevertheless, when her assailant began tugging on her purse again, she held fast.

"Let go, lady, or you'll get more of the same." The command came out in a snarl.

She maintained her viselike grip on her purse.

A second later the hard toe of a boot slammed against the

skin over her ribs, and she gasped as a searing pain shot through her side.

Moaning, she curled into a tight ball and fought the waves of blackness that swept over her.

Once again the man gripped her purse, grabbing a handful of her blouse at the same time. As he yanked, the sound of ripping fabric rent the air.

And then the world went black.

* * *

After a sleepless night and a distracted day at work, Nick pulled to a stop in front of Laura's apartment and raked his fingers through his hair.

After the enlightening weekend visit to her home town, he'd needed some time to process all he'd learned and decide on next steps.

Step one? Convince her to make another Ted Drewes run with him tonight. Maybe there, amid a crowd that would provide safety in numbers, he might be able to ferret out a few more details about her marriage that would give him a clue about why she was so scared of relationships.

Because even though the odds of breaking through her defenses were formidable, that almost-kiss in the wood told him she was as attracted to him as he was to her. He just had to convince her that whatever had gone wrong in her marriage wasn't a template for all relationships.

As he turned off the engine, he scanned the empty, dark, run-down neighborhood.

This was obviously not a place where couples and families took evening strolls.

Or was it?

A movement down the street caught his eye, but his perusal changed from idle curiosity to pulse-pounding alertness when it became apparent that a struggle was taking place. One of the two figures was lying on the sidewalk while the other—a male, based on his build—delivered a hard kick, then leaned down and attempted to grab something.

It looked like a mugging.

Reacting on instinct, Nick flung open his door and sprinted toward the man. "Hey! Back off!"

The man whirled around, and after one final, futile tug on what looked like a purse, he abandoned the attack and took off running in the opposite direction.

Nick continued forward, but as he approached the victim his pulse lost its rhythm when her identity registered.

It was Laura.

Gut twisting, he dropped to one knee beside her.

Her blouse was half torn off. Blood covered her face. One eye had already swollen shut. Her breathing was labored. And she seemed barely conscious.

Shock waves ricocheted through him until her soft moan spurred him into action.

"Laura, can you hear me?" He leaned closer and touched her shoulder

Her only response was to curl into a tighter ball.

Tempted as he was to pick her up and carry her to her apartment, that could be a mistake. Moving her could exacerbate whatever injuries she'd suffered.

Instead he pulled out his cell and tapped in 911 with a shaky finger. After giving the dispatcher all the relevant information, he did his best to stanch the flow of blood from her nose with his handkerchief, praying harder than he'd ever prayed in his life.

In the distance, a siren pierced the night air, and a couple of minutes later a police car with flashing lights turned the corner.

He stood and waved until the car rolled to a stop on the street next to him.

An officer alighted and circled the car to join him. "You the one who called this in?" He knelt beside Laura.

"Yes." Nick dropped back down on her other side as the man gave her a cursory once-over.

"This was a mugging, right?"

"Yes."

"An ambulance is on the way."

"No." Laura's eyes fluttered open, her voice a mere whisper. "No hospital."

Nick took her hand. "Laura, you need to get checked out. You could be seriously injured."

She turned her head toward him. Squinted, as if she was having trouble focusing. "Nick?"

"Yes. I'm right here."

"No hospital."

Why not?

There had to be a reason, but this wasn't the time to probe for it. His priority had to be convincing her to go.

"Look, I'll stay with you the whole time, okay? I promise. But you need to get checked out."

She drew a shuddering breath. Winced. Pressed a hand to her side. "Okay." Then her eyelids drifted closed.

Had she lost consciousness?

"Wherc's the ambulance?" He barked out the question to the officer.

"It will be here any minute. I take it you know the victim."

"Yes. I was on my way to see her. She lives in that building." He motioned toward it. "I'd just parked when I saw the attack."

"Lucky timing for her."

The faint echo of a siren keened through the air, and within minutes two paramedics were hustling over to join them. Only then did he relinquish her hand.

Her eyelids flickered open again as his fingers broke contact. "Nick?" There was a hint of panic in her voice.

"I'm here." He moved into her line of sight.

The paramedics did a quick exam, then went to retrieve the stretcher.

Once again, Nick dropped to one knee beside her. "I'll meet you at the hospital."

"Okay. Th-thank you."

While the paramedics transferred her to the stretcher, the officer motioned him aside. "I'll follow you there. I'll need a statement, since you were a witness, and hopefully the victim will be able to talk to me later. Let me get your names, though, before you leave."

Nick gave him the information, verified the hospital they were transporting her to, then strode toward his car, forcing himself to take long, slow breaths. Unless he calmed down, he could end up in an accident en route.

He did, in fact, beat the ambulance to the hospital—but trying to get back to Laura in the treatment room once she arrived proved difficult, since he wasn't family. The gatekeeper in the ER intake area was apparently a strict by-the-rules player.

"Look, just ask her if it's okay for me to come back." He wasn't in the mood to play nice, but being demanding wasn't going to win him any brownie points. So he softened his voice. "Please."

"I'll go back as soon as I have a minute."

That was the best he was going to get.

But he wasn't above enlisting the help of the cop on his tail if he was still cooling his heels in the waiting room when the officer arrived.

Fortunately, the door to the treatment area swooshed open a few minutes later and he was ushered back.

"She's in room six." The woman pointed down a hall.

"Thanks."

He jogged down the corridor, pausing at the half-open door as a woman in scrubs exited.

"You must be Nick."

"Yes."

"Go on in. The doctor will be in to see her in a couple of minutes."

Nick entered, pushing aside the curtain that had been pulled around the bed.

And almost lost his dinner.

Laura had looked bad on the street. But here, under the bright overhead lights, her injuries were fully exposed. At least the ones he could see.

The blood had been cleaned from her face, but her nose was puffy. So was her eye, which was red and half-closed. A gauze bandage was wrapped around her hand. Her blouse had been replaced by a hospital gown.

"I wouldn't win any beauty contest tonight, would I?" She tried for a smile, but couldn't quite pull it off.

His throat pinched.

After all she'd been through, she was trying to make a joke.

He moved beside her. Cocooned her icy, uninjured hand between his. "You look beautiful to me." His words came out in a rasp.

She sniffed. Swallowed. "How did you happen to be there tonight when the guy jumped me?"

"I was hoping for a Ted Drewes run. Will you give me a rain check?"

Before she could answer, the curtain swooshed open again. A woman in a white coat entered, introduced herself, and moved to Laura's side. "Let's take a look and see what we have."

As she started to lift Laura's gown, Nick backed toward the door. "I'll, uh, wait in the hall until you're finished." Then he slipped outside to give her privacy.

When the doctor came out a few minutes later, she stopped beside him. "Ms. Taylor said it was okay to fill you in. We're going to X-ray her nose and ribs. She'll likely have a black eye, but there doesn't appear to be any ocular damage. She says she didn't hit her head when she fell, and I don't feel any lumps, but she thinks she may have blacked out for a moment. I'm not seeing any neurological issues, but it's possible she has a mild concussion. The minor abrasion on her palm is nothing to worry about."

"Thanks for the update."

"No problem."

As the doctor moved on, he started to reenter the room. Paused when a scrubs-clad guy stopped beside him.

"You with the patient in this room?" The man motioned to the doorway.

"Yes."

"I'm taking her to X-ray. Could be a while. We've got a backlog."

"Thanks for the heads-up."

He followed the guy in.

Laura looked more alert now, which was good.

But the brackets around her mouth, and the taut line of her features, weren't.

She had to be hurting. Bad.

"I'll be here when you get back from X-ray." He took her hand. Gently squeezed her fingers.

"It's getting late. You don't have to stay."

"I'm in for the duration."

A sheen appeared in her eyes. "Thank you."

"No thanks necessary."

The man wheeled her out, and Nick propped a shoulder against the wall. Wiped a hand down his face.

What a night.

And it wasn't close to being over yet.

In fact, the way hospital ERs operated, it could be the wee hours before—

A knock sounded at the door, and a second later the police officer from the scene poked his head in, a cup of coffee in each hand. He held one out. "I thought you might appreciate some caffeine."

He took the cup, then gripped it with both hands as a case of the shakes set in. "Thanks."

"Why don't we find a quiet spot in the waiting room to talk?"

With a nod, he followed the officer in silence.

Once they sat, the man pulled out a notebook and angled toward him. "How's she doing?"

"TBD. She's in X-ray."

The man set his coffee on a side table and retrieved a pen

from his pocket. "Why don't you tell me what you witnessed?"

"Not much, actually. I think I came in near the end." He relayed what he'd observed while the officer took notes.

"Can you give me a description of the assailant?"

"I wish I could, but it was too dark. Besides, the guy took off before I got close enough to see anything, and he had a cap pulled low over his eyes. All I know for sure is that he had the build of a linebacker."

"Ms. Taylor may be able to add something to your description."

Nick frowned. "I'm not certain she'll be up to talking to you tonight. They also warned me it could be a while before she gets back from X-ray."

"We can put off the interview if necessary, but I'll hang around for an hour or so."

"I'm going to wait for her back there." He hooked a thumb toward the treatment rooms.

"I'll stay out here." The officer pulled out his phone and took a call.

While Nick cooled his heels and drank his coffee in Laura's room, he tried to check emails and texts. But when he sent a requested document to the wrong person, he gave up. There was no way he was going to be able to concentrate until he knew she was okay.

Sixty minutes later, the door to the room opened and the same guy wheeled Laura back in. "She's all yours."

If only.

"Thanks."

As the man exited, Nick moved beside her.

"You waited." Her lips rose a hair.

"I said I would—and I always do what I say."

"Nice to know."

"How are you feeling?"

"Like I got hit by a truck."

"Close enough." He took her hand and gave her a quick scan.

Her pallor was alarming, but so were the additional injuries he could see, now that her gown had slipped off one shoulder and exposed a broad expanse of skin. The long, angry bruise that ran down the front of her shoulder must have been inflicted by the strap of her bag—but what had caused the three-inch-long scar of older vintage a couple of inches below her right clavicle?

Before he could figure out how to diplomatically frame that question, the door swung open and the doctor entered. "Would you like your friend to stay while we discuss your condition?" She tipped her head his direction as she spoke to Laura.

"Yes."

"You're a very lucky woman, Ms. Taylor. No broken bones, and no internal injuries. You'll likely have a black eye, so I'd suggest an ice pack when you get home. The nose will be tender for a few days, but it will heal without any intervention. No broken ribs, but two are badly bruised. Over-the-counter pain meds will help with the discomfort. I'd also advise you to take it easy for a few days to give them a chance to start healing. All of this will be in the printed instructions you'll take home with you."

Laura's brow puckered. "Would it be a problem if I go back to work in a day or two?"

"I'd recommend waiting until you can move comfortably, but that's your call. I'd strongly suggest you not drive for a few days, though." She pulled out her phone. Glanced at the screen before continuing. "There's a police officer in the hall who would like to talk to you if you feel up to it."

"That's fine."

The doctor disappeared out the door, and a moment later the officer entered.

After the man introduced himself to Laura, he pulled out his notebook again, jotting as she responded to his questions.

Nick gave her fingers an encouraging squeeze while she spoke, but her details of the attack were even more vague than his.

"I wish I could tell you more." She took a slow breath. "But it happened so fast, and it was dark. All I know for sure is that the man was big and strong."

"Any idea about age or race?"

She shook her head. "No. I'm sorry."

"Do you usually walk at that time of night?"

"No. I was only out there tonight because I took the bus home late from work."

Nick frowned. "Wait a minute. I assumed you'd just parked up the street and were walking to your apartment. What happened to your truck? I thought you were picking it up tonight."

"It wasn't ready."

"Then why didn't you call me for a ride?"

"Mr. Sinclair." The officer arched an eyebrow at him. "I have a few more questions."

Nick blew out a breath. "Sorry."

The man attempted to elicit a few more details from Laura, but to no avail.

"I suppose there isn't much chance of catching him, is there?" She bunched the sheet in her fingers.

"Honestly? Almost none." He closed his notebook. "He didn't get your purse, did he?"

"No. I kept a tight grip on it."

"Let me leave you with one piece of advice. I hope this never happens to you again, but if it does, let your purse go. Your life is worth more than whatever is in there. That man could have had a gun or a knife, and if he had, you might be in the morgue instead of here." He fished out a card and handed it to her. "If you think of anything else, give me a call."

Silence fell as the man exited.

He may have been a bit blunt, but Nick couldn't argue with anything he'd said. "He's right, you know. Losing a purse is far better than losing your life."

Laura's features hardened. "I won't let anyone take what's mine. I won't be a victim again."

What did that mean?

Before he could follow up, she swallowed. Squeezed his fingers. "Take me home. Please."

He nodded. His questions could wait until later. Laura had had all the stress she could take for one day. "I'll find the nurse and see if I can speed up your discharge."

Within ten minutes, an aide was helping Laura dress while he went in search of her discharge paperwork.

He was waiting in the hall when the aide brought her out in a wheelchair. She was wearing an oversized surgical top instead of her blouse, which had no doubt been damaged beyond repair, and she was holding her side. Her face also had an alarming gray cast.

The mere act of standing and dressing must have been beyond painful.

Yet somehow she managed to dredge up a smile for him. "I bet you're past ready to ditch this place."

His throat clogged. "I'd have stayed all night if necessary."

A faint tinge of pink mitigated the ashen hue of her cheeks.

"Well I, for one, am ready to go home."

"Then let's get out of here."

But home wasn't his final destination tonight. At least not *her* home.

And as he left the ER to retrieve his car, he prepared to dig in his heels if she wasn't receptive to his plan.

10

The last few hours had been surreal.

As Laura eased into Nick's car, trying not to wince, she gritted her teeth.

All she wanted to do was go home, take a painkiller, and crawl into bed. The sooner the better.

Once she was settled, Nick rounded the hood and slid behind the wheel. Looked over at her. "Do you need help with the seat belt?"

"I can't wear it tonight." The mere thought of even a tiny amount of pressure on her aching ribs made her queasy.

"I'll take it extra slow going home. And speaking of home…" He put the car in gear and pulled away from the ER entrance. "I'd like you to stay at my place tonight."

She did a double take. "Why?"

"Because I don't think you should be alone, especially with a possible concussion. And unless your couch is a sofa bed, there's no place for me to sleep at your apartment."

"It's not a sofa bed."

"Then stay at my condo. Please. Otherwise, I'll end up sleeping on your floor."

It was hard to refuse when he put it like that.

And truth be told, it would be comforting to have someone close by tonight. Sam would come, of course, if she called her—

but why ruin anyone else's evening at this late hour?

"Do you have a guest room?"

"No. But I do have a sofa bed."

Not ideal, but better than being alone.

"Okay."

He sent her a surprised glance as he guided the car through the dark night. As if he'd expected her to refuse.

And maybe, in the light of day, she'd wish she had.

But right now, she was going to follow her instincts.

"Good. Unless there's something you need at your apartment, I'd rather go straight home. I have extra toothbrushes, and you could use one of my T-shirts to sleep in."

"That works." Because with every minute that passed, the torture of sitting in his car grew exponentially, despite the comfortable leather seats. A detour to her apartment would only prolong the agony.

He studied her in the dim light, forehead crinkling. "I know you're hurting, but hang in. We'll be there in ten minutes."

Bracing herself against the door, she tried to stay as still as possible. But despite Nick's careful driving, every bump, every turn, sent a shaft of pain through her rib cage.

When they finally arrived, she had to blink to clear the moisture from her vision.

"Sit tight and I'll help you out." Nick set the brake, turned off the engine, and circled the car.

When he opened the passenger door and extended a hand, she bit her lip.

Getting out of the car was going to hurt.

A lot.

So was the walk to his condo.

But when there was no other choice, you did what you had to do.

Mashing her lips together, she took his hand.

Hard as she tried, she couldn't bite back her gasp when he drew her to her feet. And once upright, she sagged against the door. "Sorry." The word wobbled.

After giving her a worried scan, he touched her cheek. "Wait here." Then he disappeared.

Just when her legs were about to buckle, he reappeared. "If I had the transporter from the Enterprise, I'd beam you up to my second floor. But this is the next best thing." Before she realized his intent, he bent and lifted her into his arms, cradling her uninjured side against his chest.

She should object. After all, she was used to standing on her own two feet.

But somehow her ribs didn't hurt quite as much with the steady beat of his heart beneath her ear. So she remained silent.

Moving with utmost care, he carried her up the path and through the open door of his condo, continued up a flight of stairs, and walked down a dark hall. When he entered the room at the end, he flicked on a light with his elbow, then lowered her to a firm mattress.

She released a long, slow breath.

"I'm going to fix an ice pack for your eye and get you a painkiller. Just sit here until I get back."

"I don't plan to move a muscle."

And she didn't.

In fact, if she could stay just like this all night, she'd be happy.

But he was back much too fast, the promised T-shirt over his arm, juggling a glass of water in one hand and the ice bag in the other. He set the water and ice bag on the nightstand, then handed her two pills.

She swallowed them with a long sip of water. The sooner they kicked in, the better.

"Will this work to sleep in?" He held up the T-shirt, which sported a Cardinals baseball logo.

"I think I'll get lost in it, but yes, that will be fine. I can change while you make up the sofa bed for me."

"Correction. You're sleeping here. I'll take the sofa."

"No way." She shook her head.

"Yes, way. Besides, I just changed these sheets this morning. I got up super early and decided to do a few chores. It was lucky timing."

Laura thought about arguing—then thought better of it. The less moving around the better at this stage, and real beds were always more comfortable than sleeper sofas. A huge consideration tonight.

"I'll owe you for this."

"Nope. The offer comes with no strings attached." He detoured to the attached bath. "I'll put fresh towels on the vanity for you, along with a new toothbrush. My dentist gives me one at every visit." His voice was muffled as drawers opened and the knob of a door rattled. Then he was back. "I'll go make up the sofa bed. Just call out to me when you're set."

He left the room, closing the door behind him.

For a full minute, Laura remained seated on the side of the bed. But at last she maneuvered herself to her feet and shuffled toward the bathroom, holding onto her side with one hand and the furniture she passed with the other.

When she reached the bathroom and turned toward the mirror over the sink, her stomach flipped.

Sweet mercy.

She was an absolute, total mess.

Her ponytail was askew, her eye was red and swollen half shut, and lines of pain scored her forehead and the corners of her mouth.

Dare she look at her ribs?

Catching her lower lip between her teeth, she gingerly worked up the surgical top. Stopped breathing as she stared at the blue-black contusion across her midsection.

And the bruise down the front of her shoulder must be from her purse strap.

After wadding the surgical top into a ball, she gave her teeth a cursory brushing and used the toilet—even if getting up and down taxed her endurance to the limit.

Now all she had to do was put on the T-shirt and get her jeans off.

Donning the shirt wasn't that difficult once she returned to the bedroom, but the jeans were a different story. So were her sport shoes. She managed to tug the jeans down past her hips, but bending over was excruciating.

Now what?

"Everything okay in there?"

At Nick's query, she eased onto the side of the bed. "Um…I have a little problem."

"May I come in?"

"Yes."

He pushed the door open and crossed the room, twin furrows etched on his brow. "What's wrong?"

"I can't get my shoes or my jeans off. Bending over hurts too much."

"Lucky thing I'm here, then." He flashed her a grin. "Let's start with the shoes."

As he dropped to one knee in front of her, she tugged down

the hem of the T-shirt. But since it came almost to her knees, there weren't really any modesty issues.

He untied her shoes, loosened the laces, and gently eased her feet out of them. "You want the socks off too?"

"Yes, please."

He peeled off the first one, lips bowing as he cradled her foot in his hand. "Nice pedicure."

Huh.

Most guys didn't pay attention to such things.

Then again, Nick didn't seem to be like most guys.

"My one concession to vanity. I've always envied women with beautiful nails, but those aren't practical in my line of work. This is the next best thing. It's good for my ego, if nothing else." Warmth crept across her cheeks. "It's kind of silly, I guess."

"On the contrary. I think it's charming. And everyone deserves a bit of pampering."

"I don't go to a salon or anything." In case he thought she spent her hard-earned dollars on frivolities. "I'm not very good at painting them, but no one sees them except me. Or they didn't until tonight."

"Your secret is safe with me." He dispensed with her other sock and moved on to the jeans, easing them down her legs and setting them on a chair by the wall. "Done." He stood.

"Thanks." She started to lie down, and he instantly bent, supporting her shoulders and lifting her legs.

"You have a good bedside manner." Her words slurred as weariness settled over her and her eyelids grew heavy.

"Try to keep this on your eye." When he gently settled the ice bag against her tender skin, she winced at the weight and the cold.

"I will." She lifted a hand to hold it in place.

"I'll be right outside if you need anything."

"'kay." She gave up trying to keep her eyes open.

But in the moments before she drifted into welcome oblivion, a most pleasant whisper of warmth trailed across her forehead.

* * *

Something was wrong.

Struggling to kick-start his brain, Nick tried to orient himself.

Oh, yeah.

He was sleeping in the sofa bed in the loft that overlooked his living room.

Because Laura was in *his* bed.

Cocking his ear toward the closed door of his bedroom, he listened.

Total silence.

Yet something had awakened him.

He groped for his phone on the table beside him and scanned the screen. Stifled a groan as the time came into focus.

Three-thirty.

No wonder he was groggy. Two hours of sleep weren't nearly enough.

He settled back against the pillow, and when all remained quiet he let himself drift off again.

Until a very distinctive, if muffled, sound registered.

A woman was sobbing.

His brain snapped to attention, all fuzziness evaporating.

A second later, he swung his feet to the floor, sped across the loft, and cracked the door to the bedroom.

The dim nightlight provided only marginal illumination, but he could see enough to get the lay of the land. Laura was in the throes of a nightmare, thrashing around on the bed and mumbling incoherently between her sobs.

No surprise, after all she'd been through last night.

He entered and moved beside her, but as he reached down to awaken her, she flung out an arm.

"No, Joe, don't! Please don't hurt me!"

As her panicked words registered, Nick sucked in a breath.

She wasn't having a nightmare about last night's attacker.

She was having a nightmare about her husband.

As her thrashing grew more intense, Nick gently grasped her upper arms. If she didn't calm down, she could exacerbate her injuries. "It's okay, Laura. It's okay."

He continued murmuring the assurance in a soothing voice until at last her eyelids flickered open. "Nick?"

"Yeah. You had a bad dream."

A shudder rippled through her. "I'm sorry I w-woke you."

"No worries. Just relax and try to go back to sleep. Would you like me to stay until you drift off?"

Despite the dim light, the indecision on her face was easy to read. And it wasn't hard to decipher it. She wanted him to stay, but didn't want to further disrupt his night.

Linking his fingers with hers, he sat on the edge of the bed and took the decision out of her hands. "I'll stay for a few minutes."

"You must be exhausted. It has to be the middle of the night." Her protest was halfhearted at best.

"I'm wide awake."

He was prepared to cajole if necessary, but she gave up the fight—and her capitulation spoke volumes about how bad her nightmare had been.

A nightmare about her husband, who'd obviously hurt her physically as well as emotionally.

After a few minutes her respiration evened out and her grip on his fingers loosened, but as she relaxed he grew *more* tense.

What kind of monster had she married? How badly had he hurt her? Was the older-vintage scar he'd noticed tonight in the ER connected to her husband?

Rage began to simmer deep in his gut.

How could anyone harm this caring, principled, hard-working, conscientious woman who loved her family and believed in helping those who needed a hand up?

But if she'd been in an abusive marriage, it was no wonder she was gun-shy of relationships and had difficulty with trust.

When she seemed to be in a peaceful slumber, Nick extricated his hand and stood. He ought to go back to bed.

But what if she woke up again in the grip of another nightmare?

Scrubbing a hand down his face, he sank into the overstuffed chair near the bed. Let his head drop onto the cushioned back. Stared at the dark ceiling.

It had been a long day—and it was going to be a long night…what little remained of it. With all the questions swirling through his mind, the odds of him getting much more shut-eye were minuscule. Especially after the shocking reveal in her nightmare.

If the man she'd loved had abused her, that legacy could be a formidable hurdle to overcome. And until she told him more about what had happened to her, he was running blind.

The time had come to ask some hard questions. Talk about the baggage that weighed her down. That was the only way forward.

Because until they confronted the demons from her past, they had no hope of a future together.

* * *

Where was she?

As Laura surfaced from a deep sleep, brain sluggish, she squinted at the unfamiliar setting in the pale light peeking around the blinds on the window.

A window she didn't recognize.

She started to roll onto her back, but at the sharp pain in her side she froze as all the events of the night before came roaring back.

She'd been injured in a mugging. And she was in Nick's condo. In his bed.

Moving with the utmost caution, she managed to turn onto her back.

Froze again when she spotted Nick in the adjacent chair.

He was out cold, head tipped back, fingers linked over his stomach, legs stretched in front of him. His hair was tousled, his jaw bristly, and his feet were bare beneath his sweatpants.

But it was the snug T-shirt that emphasized his broad shoul ders and muscled chest that caught—and held—her attention.

Staring at a person who was sleeping felt almost like an invasion of privacy, however. She ought to turn away or speak to him so he woke up and—

Too late.

His eyelids snapped open, almost as if he'd sensed her perusal, and he straightened up. "Good morning." His greeting came out in a sleep-roughened voice that sent a little tingle racing through her.

She ignored the sensation. "Did you sleep there all night?"

One side of his mouth quirked up. "What little was left of it." He twisted his neck, as if he was trying to unkink it. "How do you feel?"

"Sore. But I'll be okay, thanks to you."

"I wish I'd been five minutes sooner."

"I'm just glad you weren't five minutes later. What time is it?"

He twisted his wrist. "Six-thirty."

"I need to call my foreman. He was supposed to pick me up today."

Nick stood. "Is your phone in your purse?"

"Yes."

He crossed the room, plucked her bag off the dresser, and carried it back. "Would you like me to help you sit up?" He set the purse on the bed beside her.

"I think it may be less painful if I maneuver myself upright."

"In that case, why don't I go get you another dose of pain medicine while you make your call?"

Music to her ears.

"I'd appreciate that."

As soon as he exited, she managed to sit up and swing her legs to the floor with only a few grunts and groans. Then she dug out her cell, filled Ken in on the situation, and inched her way to the bathroom.

By the time she returned, Nick was waiting with a glass of water and two more pills. He'd also changed from his sweatpants and T into chinos and a cotton shirt with the sleeves rolled to the elbows.

She took the pills from him in silence and downed them in one gulp. "Thank you."

"You're welcome. Why don't you try to get some more sleep? It's still early."

"No. I should go home. I can rest there. Would you mind dropping me off on the way to your office?"

"I'm not planning to go in today."

She blinked. "Why not?"

"I'd rather spend the day with you. Here."

"But…I'm sure you have a busy schedule."

"Jack can cover for me."

Tempted as she was to let him pamper her all day, she shook her head. "No. I wrecked your evening last night. I don't want to disrupt your workday too."

He hiked up one side of his mouth. "Look at it this way. You gave me an excuse to play hooky. Unless you don't want my company."

Oh, she wanted his company. Too much, in fact. Which was why she should insist he go to work and take her home.

But maybe, just this once, she could be selfish.

Because at the moment, spending the day with him sounded like the next best thing to Christmas.

Besides, she really wasn't up to moving around, and having a few more hours to veg and heal before she dived back into her routine would be wonderful. Not that she'd be up to field work for the next couple of weeks, but she had plenty of design projects to keep her busy.

"As a matter of fact, I'd enjoy your company if you can spare the time."

"I'd *make* the time for you any day."

The warmth in his eyes sent a shaft of heat straight to her core, and she cleared her throat. Edged toward the bed. "I, uh, think I'll take your advice and sleep for another couple of hours, if that's okay."

"Fine by me. I'll tackle my inbox and take care of a few chores."

He waited until she slid back under the covers before he left, quietly closing the door behind him.

As she lay in the bed, waiting for the pain pills to kick in, she faced the simple truth that she'd been dodging for weeks, impossible to evade in light of Nick's willingness to go the extra mile for her after last night's incident.

He was special. The kind of man who seemed authentic in every way.

And she was falling hard.

But what if she was wrong about him? What if she let herself get too involved, only to discover her judgment had failed her once again?

She'd survived the last time, but she couldn't go through that again.

And the only way to eliminate that risk was to keep Nick—and all men—at arm's length.

Even if the thought of walking away from the man outside her door made her sick to her stomach.

11

Three hours later, when the sounds of stirring came from the bedroom, Nick set his laptop next to him on the sleeper sofa that was now a couch again, stood, and crossed to the closed door. Gave a soft knock. "Laura? Are you up?"

"Yes." Her muffled voice sounded stronger than it had last night. "You can come in."

He twisted the knob and entered.

She was sitting on the edge of the bed, looking battered but more rested and alert.

"Did you sleep?"

"Like a rock."

"Are you hungry?"

"Yes. I missed dinner last night, and my stomach is reminding me of that. A bowl of cereal or a piece of toast would be great, if you have either."

"I think I can do better than that. My fridge contents are on the lean side, but I do have eggs."

She shook her head. "You don't have to cook for me, Nick."

"I'll be cooking for me too. I haven't eaten breakfast yet either. Besides, you may be sorry I *did* cook once you sample my efforts."

Her lips twitched. "I doubt that will happen. At this stage, K-rations would taste good. But would you mind if I took a shower first? I feel grungy."

"Be my guest. There's soap and shampoo in dispensers in there."

"This is better than a first-class hotel."

"I'd ask you to leave me a good review on Tripadvisor, but these accommodations are reserved for very special guests."

"In that case, I'm honored."

"I'll leave you to your shower. Do you need any more clothes?"

"I don't think so. This T-shirt is long enough to be a dress. It will be fine until I go home."

He walked back to the door. "Do you feel up to coming downstairs to eat, or would you like me to bring the food up here?"

"Downstairs will be fine."

"Call me when you're ready and I'll help you down the steps. Do you need anything else before I don my chef hat?"

"No. But the shower could take me a while. I'm moving slow."

"I'll listen for the water to go off before I dive into breakfast prep. Be careful."

"No worries on that score. Caution is my middle name. I do *not* need any more bruises."

"Agreed." He left her, closed the door behind him, and headed downstairs to see what he could rummage up in his understocked kitchen.

By the time he set the table, planned his menu, and got out the ingredients for their simple breakfast, the shower was going.

It went off much faster than he'd expected, however, so he moved into high gear on the breakfast prep.

Just as the scrambled eggs began to set, Laura appeared in

the kitchen doorway.

He angled toward her, keeping an eye on the eggs. She was barefoot, and her damp hair hung long over her shoulders as she held onto the doorframe. In contrast to the usual strong image she tried to project, she looked vulnerable and fragile. And even with her shiner and puffy nose, she was the most appealing woman he'd ever met.

But she shouldn't have tackled the steps alone.

"I thought you were going to call me when you were ready to come down."

"I wanted to make sure I could manage the steps. After all, I'll be on my own once you take me home."

That was true.

Even if he'd prefer to hang close until she was fully recovered.

"Go ahead and have a seat." He motioned to the table. "I put two more pills and a glass of water in your place."

She crossed to it, her gait slow and shuffling, one hand pressed to her side. Biting her lower lip, she lowered herself into a chair, then downed the two pills with a long swallow of water.

That, and her pallor, confirmed that she was still in serious pain.

"Sorry about the wet hair." She fluffed it with her hand. "I didn't want to go rooting around in your vanity for a blow-dryer."

"I wouldn't have minded. I'll get it for you after we eat." He dished up the eggs, pulled the bagel halves from the toaster, and carried their plates to the table. "It's not gourmet, but it will fill the empty place."

When she looked down at the plate he set in front of her, her breath hitched. "You even peeled the orange for me."

"It was the least I could do to fancy up a pretty ordinary breakfast."

She lifted her gaze to his, irises shimmering. "It's not ordinary to me. It's been a long time since I felt so t-taken care of."

At the catch in her voice, his throat thickened.

Truth be told, he'd like to take care of her forever—an odd reaction for a guy who'd played the field all his life. Yet he didn't mind in the least.

It was way too soon to say anything like that to Laura, though. Such an admission could scare her off.

Giving her a wink, he kept his tone light. "Add that to your Tripadvisor review." And for the remainder of the meal he kept the conversation on impersonal topics.

Once they finished, he cleared the table, retrieved the blow-dryer for her, and cleaned up their dishes while she dried her hair.

When she reappeared, he draped the dish towel over the sink and propped his hands on his hips. "Would you like to watch a movie? I'll even bite the bullet and agree to a rom-com, if that's your preference."

She smiled. "I appreciate that offer, but I'm fine with a mystery or suspense."

"Classic or modern?"

"Honestly? I prefer the classic movies. They're cleaner."

"How about North by Northwest?"

"One of my favorites."

They moved to the living room, and after he called the film up on his TV he joined her on the couch. "You doing okay?"

"As long as I don't move too much or breathe too heavy."

He scrutinized her. Much as he wanted to broach the subject of her nightmare, he held back. Her pallor was still unsettling, and she likely wasn't up to such a heavy discussion. He'd told her once he was patient. This was the time to demonstrate that.

But maybe he could flex that rule just a bit on a different front, since they were sitting side-by-side.

Slowly he reached over. Wove his fingers with hers. "Will this make you breathe too heavy?" He lifted their clasped hands.

She moistened her lips. "Maybe. But I'll take the trade-off."

That was the most encouraging news he'd had all week.

After giving her fingers a squeeze, he started the film—and for two-plus hours, he held her hand. That was far less than he'd done with other women who'd shared this couch with him for a movie, but it had a much bigger impact on his heart.

Just as the closing credits began to roll, his cell started vibrating on the coffee table.

When he ignored it, Laura glanced at him. "Aren't you going to answer that?"

"I'd prefer not to."

"It could be important."

"You're more important." But when he gave the screen a quick scan and saw Jack's name, he frowned. After the download he'd given him this morning, his partner wouldn't call unless something serious had come up.

Laura freed her fingers. "Go ahead and answer it. I can see Jack's name from here. Don't neglect your business on my account."

Expelling a breath, he picked up the phone. "What's up?"

"Sorry to bother you, buddy, but Andrew White called. He wants to stop by at one-thirty to review our progress on his office building."

"You can handle that. You're up to date."

"I know. But it's your project—and I've got a two o'clock

with the Chesterfield planning department guy to answer his questions about the Anderson house."

Nick massaged his temples. That municipality had been giving them fits about the megamansion Jack had designed, and trying to keep both the city and the Andersons happy had been a pain in the tush.

"Can you move your meeting?"

"Dicey. Our contact there is going on vacation tomorrow for two weeks, and I'd prefer not to start over with someone new."

"I could call Andrew and see if he'd be willing to meet with me tomorrow instead of today." But his client wouldn't be happy about that. With all his clout, the man was used to people jumping when he said jump.

"Nick." Laura touched his arm.

"Hold a sec, Jack." He muted the phone and turned to her.

"Go to your meeting. It sounds important. And there's no sense in both of us falling behind in our work. You can drop me at my apartment on the way to your office."

Blast.

This wasn't how his day was supposed to go.

But in truth, Laura didn't need him. She'd be fine on her own for the afternoon. And asking Jack to scramble to cover for him was selfish.

He unmuted the phone. "I'll be there."

"Okay. I wouldn't have called if I wasn't between a rock and a hard place."

"I know."

"Tell Laura I said hi."

"Will do." He ended the call and angled toward her. "Jack sends his best."

"He's a good guy."

"I agree. But I have a demanding—and influential—client who's insisting on an impromptu meeting at one-thirty, and Jack has his own issue to deal with." He stood. "I need to change. Why don't you just stay here for the afternoon?"

"No. I have to go home sooner or later."

He propped his hands on his hips. "I'll tell you what. If you'll turn on your air, I'll bring Chinese for us tonight for dinner." But the air was for her, not him. With as much pain as she was in, a sweltering apartment would only intensify her discomfort.

She hiked up her eyebrows. "Is that a bribe?"

"Did it work?"

She exhaled. "Yes. I may start using the air more now, anyway. It's hard to get out of the frugal mindset I've had for so long, but with all the business that's coming in, I can afford to indulge."

"Good to hear. Give me ten minutes. I'll bring your stuff down with me when I come."

He managed to change in eight minutes, then collected her purse, shoes and socks, and jeans before rejoining her in the living room.

"I should probably try to put those back on." She nodded to the jeans. "I hate to take your shirt home."

"You can keep it if you want." He grinned. "It looks a lot better on you than it does on me. But you will need these." He lifted the shoes and socks. "Why don't I play Prince Charming?" He dropped to one knee and put them on for her, easing them on carefully and tying the laces.

When he looked up and caught the unguarded yearning in her eyes, his spirits ticked up.

She might not think she was ready to let anyone into her

heart, but this was another sign he was making inroads.

He stood and held out his hand. "Want an assist?"

"Yes. I think I'll need it getting up from this couch. It's kind of low-slung."

She placed her fingers in his, and he gently drew her to her feet. Once she was steady, he took a step back. "Let me grab my laptop and we'll be set to go."

The drive to her apartment took longer than he expected, thanks to an accident that tied up traffic. So although he'd have preferred to linger when he dropped her off, the clock was ticking on his meeting with Andrew. And his client wouldn't be nearly as gracious about being kept waiting as Laura had been the day he was tardy for their initial meeting.

"You'll take it easy this afternoon, right?" He paused in the hall outside her door once they ascended the steps to her apartment.

"I won't have much choice. I left my laptop at my office."

"Do you want me to get it for you on my way back here later?"

"I appreciate that, but Sam's in that area a lot, and she has a key. She may be able to swing by and grab it."

"Let me know if that doesn't work out."

"I will." She swallowed. "Thank you for all your help."

He shoved one hand in his pocket. "Aside from the circumstances that prompted it, being with you was a pleasure." His words came out husky.

She moistened her lips as he gazed at her without making any attempt to mask his attraction.

"Well..." She eased back a step. "You should get to work."

Yeah, he should.

Even if he hated to leave her here alone.

"I'll text you when I'm on my way back. Call if you need anything."

"I'll be fine."

With a nod, he turned away and hustled down the steps.

But he'd be counting the hours until he returned.

And hoping that Laura would recognize soon that he posed no threat to her—and that she'd give him a chance to prove just how much he cared about her.

* * *

"Hey, kiddo. What's up?"

As Sam answered her phone, Laura tried without much success to find a more comfortable position on her couch. "Quite a bit, as a matter of fact. For starters, I was mugged last night."

The sound of a sharply indrawn breath came over the line. "Are you okay?"

"I have a few injuries." She gave her a quick laundry list. "But I'd be a lot worse off if Nick hadn't shown up before the attack escalated."

A beat ticked by. "How on earth did that providential timing come about?"

"He said he had a trip to Ted Drewes in mind."

Sam snorted. "Trust me. He had a lot more on his mind than frozen custard if he came to your place after a long day at work. Kudos to him for being the knight in shining armor."

"Let's not get carried away." Even if she'd had the exact same thought.

"Hey. A girl can dream, can't she? How long did he stick around?"

This was where it was going to get sticky.

"He followed the ambulance to the hospital. When they discharged me, he said he didn't want me to spend the night by myself because of the possible concussion. Since I didn't want him to have to sleep on my couch, I went with his alternate suggestion."

"Which was…?"

"Spend the night at his place."

More silence.

Laura waited her out.

"Let me get this straight." Sam's voice was cautious. "You spent the night at a man's condo. Just you and him."

"Yes."

"Where did you sleep?"

"In his bed. He slept on the sofa sleeper."

"Wow." Sam's voice was hushed. "This is a huge step forward. If you trusted him enough to spend a night at his place, you must be falling for him."

"Or maybe I was too upset from the mugging to be thinking straight."

"You tell me. Which one was it?"

Leave it to Sam to home in on the key question.

May as well tell the truth. If you couldn't confide in your best friend, who *could* you confide in?

Laura picked up a throw pillow. Hugged it against her aching ribs. "I think I'm falling for him."

"Woo-hoo! Now you need to encourage him."

"I stayed at his place, didn't I?"

"He might have assumed what you just said—that your brain was muddled after the attack. You need to give him some direct encouragement. The kind that involves some up-close-and-personal action."

She plucked at a loose thread on the pillow. "I'm still scared."

"Nick strikes me as a patient man. My instincts tell me that if he thinks you're willing to explore the attraction, he'll play by your rules."

Yeah. That was more or less what he'd already told her.

"I'm just afraid that once I give him the green light, things may accelerate too fast."

"Then give him a yellow light. I bet he'll respect that. Has he even tried to kiss you yet?"

"No."

"See? He has self-discipline. Because believe me, he has kissing on his mind. I saw the look in his eyes that night at the bar. So it might be time to give him the green light for *that* step."

True—despite the sudden kaleidoscope of butterflies in her stomach at the mere thought of his lips on hers.

"I'll consider your suggestion. And now I have a favor to ask. Is there any way you could swing by my office and get my laptop? I also need to pick up my truck from the garage in the next few days. I'd ask Nick to take me when I'm up to driving, but I've already imposed enough."

"Laptop, no problem. As for your truck, I doubt Nick would mind helping you with that, but I'll be happy to swing by when you're ready and give you a lift to the garage."

"You're the best."

"Not even close."

Typical self-deprecating Sam.

"I beg to differ."

"We'll have to agree to disagree on that one. Did you tell your mom about the mugging?"

"No. She worries about me too much as it is. And with all

the help you and Nick are giving me, there isn't anything I need."

"Speaking of help, what's your preference on the laptop—tonight or tomorrow morning?"

"Either is fine. Nick's bringing Chinese tonight for dinner, but you're welcome to—"

"I'll stop by in the morning. Never let it be said that Sam Reynolds interfered with romance."

"There's no real romance yet."

"You need to fix that. Maybe even as soon as tonight. Kiddo, any man who goes the extra mile like Nick has for you is a keeper. And no matter how patient he is, if you keep him dangling too long he could slip away. You owe it to yourself to test the waters."

"I'll think about that."

"Don't think too long. And remember that actions speak louder than words. I'll call you tomorrow before I come. And rest today. Maybe even take a nap."

"I may do that."

But long after she ended the call with Sam, she remained on the couch.

Her best friend was right.

Nick had done everything in his power to show her he was a man of honor who was worthy of her trust.

So maybe it was time to take the first step into romance.

If she could muster up her courage before he stopped by tonight.

* * *

As Nick finished making a few notes after his lengthy meeting with Andrew, Jack stuck his head into his office, laptop in hand. "Sorry again that I couldn't fill in for you today with Andrew."

"No worries. How did your meeting go?"

He grimaced. "Mr. Nit-picky is driving me bonkers. He did more opining than a politician in election year. But I'll figure out how to address all his comments without ticking off the Andersons."

"I have great faith in your abilities and diplomacy."

"I'm glad *you* do." He propped a shoulder against the doorframe. "How was your meeting with Andrew?"

"I think he's a clone of your Mr. Nit-picky."

Jack rolled his eyes. "I guess this is what happens when you're making the big bucks, right?"

"The big bucks make the hassles easier to take."

"Tell me about it. How's Laura?"

"Beat up and hurting. I'm heading over there with take-out as soon as I can clear a few things off my desk."

"Seems like this is getting serious. First you spend the holiday weekend with her family. Now she spends the night at your place. That sounds—"

"Wait." Nick frowned and held up his hand, palm forward. "Just to clarify, she slept in my bed and I slept on the sofa sleeper. She was in no condition to do anything but rest. Besides, she has some serious trust issues when it comes to men."

"Why?"

"I'm not sure yet, but I'm beginning to get some clues."

Jack's expression grew serious. "Women with trauma in their past can be a challenge."

"I know. But she's worth it."

"You do realize that if she's been hurt once, she can be more easily hurt again."

At the cautionary note in Jack's voice, Nick let out a breath. Maybe he should be annoyed by his partner's implication, but the truth was he did have a reputation for playing the field. And how could he be upset about Jack's concern for Laura?

"Yes. And I'm not intending to hurt her. It's early in the game to know how it's going to play out, but let's just say I have no interest in seeing anyone else anymore." He leaned back in his chair. Rolled his pen between his fingers. "How did you know Melissa was The One?"

Eyebrows peaking, Jack entered and dropped into the chair across the desk. "I'd say your intentions are serious if you're asking those kinds of questions."

"That would be a fair assessment." Why pretend otherwise with his best friend?

"Okay." Jack pursed his lips. "Here are a few questions to start with when you're trying to figure out if someone is The One. How would I feel if she disappeared from my life tomorrow? Do I want to wake up next to this woman for the next fifty years? When I'm with her, do I feel like I've come home?"

Easy answers.

Terrible, yes, and yes.

"You didn't mention attraction."

Jack shrugged. "That's a given, or you wouldn't be interested in the first place. But take it from a ten-year veteran of marriage, of all the things that will keep you together long-term, attraction is down the list. Because when bills and colicky kids and backed-up plumbing in the middle of the night and all the other challenges every couple faces start to hit, you better have more than the hots for someone if you want your marriage to last. Unless you're compatible on a host of levels and committed to honoring those vows you take before God, it won't last." He grinned. "Not that the hots aren't important, of course. They can help grease the wheels through sticky patches." He stood. "And that, my son, is my wisdom for the day."

"I'll take all that to heart. But like I said, we're still in the early stages." In fact, if Jack knew he was falling this hard without ever having kissed Laura, there would be no end to his partner's ribbing.

Especially in light of his serial, no-strings dating history.

"Good luck." Jack strolled back to the door. "And keep me in the loop. It's kind of fun to see you fall hook, line, and sinker."

Fun for Jack, maybe. Not so much for him, since up to this point Laura hadn't given him a ton of encouragement.

But maybe that would change if he hung in.

A man could hope, anyway.

12

Two hours later, after wrapping up at the office, Nick texted Laura he was en route, ordered their take-out dinner, and drove back into the city.

When he reached the door of her apartment, she opened it before he could knock.

Hitching up one side of his mouth, he lowered his hand. "Were you watching for me?"

"Yes. I…I missed you."

O-kay.

That was direct. And new.

He gave her a sweep.

She'd styled her hair the way she'd worn it at the arts center groundbreaking, in long, loose waves around her shoulders. She'd also put on makeup. There wasn't much she could do to disguise the black-and-blue eye, but she'd tried to cover up the worst of the damage and added mascara to the lashes of her other eye. Her lips bore a rosy shade of gloss. And her sundress was femininity personified—and much more appealing than the baggy Cardinals T-shirt she'd been wearing earlier.

In other words, she'd dressed up for him.

Something had changed.

And unless he was misreading her cues, she was open to a greeting that was more than a simple, verbal hello

He smiled. "Likewise. In fact, I might be bold enough to demonstrate how *much* I've missed you if your face wasn't so bruised." Why not throw that out and see how she reacted? Gauge whether his read of the situation was correct?

Her throat worked. "My lips are okay."

His take was spot-on.

Pulse accelerating, he crimped the take-out bag in his fingers, bent down, and brushed his lips over hers, lingering for a few seconds when she leaned into the kiss.

This was definitely progress.

When he straightened up, soft color had bloomed on her cheeks. "You look beautiful tonight."

At his husky comment, she shook her head. "Not with a puffy nose and bruised eye, but I appreciate the thought. Come in." She waved him through the door.

He stepped over the threshold, into blessed coolness. "It feels great in here."

"I know. I should have caved sooner." She shut the door and motioned to the bag in his hand. "That smells good. I already set the table."

"Then let's eat."

He followed her into the kitchen, where they each helped themselves to generous portions of chicken broccoli and seafood delight.

While they ate, he kept the conversation focused on general topics. But if he got half a chance before their evening together ended, he was going to see what he could find out about her marriage. Because after her nightmare, it was clear her private demons were powerful. And the best way to fight an enemy was to know as much as possible about them.

After they finished their meal, he rose and started clearing the dishes.

"Let me do that." She stood too. "You provided the food. The least I can do is clean up."

"Not tonight." He continued picking up plates and utensils. "There isn't much, anyway. Why don't you wait for me in the living room?"

"You're going to spoil me."

"You could do with some spoiling." He locked gazes with her for a moment, then tipped his head toward the living room. "I'll join you in less than five minutes."

She hesitated, but in the end capitulated. "Thank you."

The minimal clean-up took little effort, and when he finished he found her sitting on the couch.

He sat beside her, lacing his fingers with hers as he scrutinized her.

The faint shadows beneath her lashes that makeup couldn't hide, along with the slight droop of her eyelids, suggested fatigue was setting in.

Much as he'd like to linger, he should leave and let her rest.

"Did you take a nap today?"

She shrugged. "I tried, but I'm not used to sleeping during the day."

"You should make it an early night."

"That's my plan."

"Will you be okay here by yourself? I could stay if that would help you sleep better."

"No. You need to get some rest yourself. I'll be fine. After all, I have to stay by myself eventually. It would just be postponing the inevitable. The memory of the attack will fade in time."

Maybe this was the opening he'd been hoping for.

"That's true." He stroked his thumb over the back of her hand, choosing his words with care. "But at the moment I'm more concerned about other memories."

Her forehead puckered. "What do you mean?"

"Laura, the nightmare you had last night wasn't about the attack. It was about Joe."

She sucked in a breath. Swallowed. "Wh-what did I say?"

"You were pleading with him not to hurt you." With his free hand, Nick reached up and touched the spot below her collarbone where he'd spotted the jagged white line. "I saw this scar at the hospital. Did he do that to you?" It took every ounce of his self-control to maintain an even tone.

Her shoulders stiffened. "What happened between Joe and me is in the past. Let's leave it there."

"I'd like to, but it's not really in the past because it's still affecting your life. And it's coming between us now. In the present. It would help me to know the history I'm up against. To understand why you're so terrified of commitment and so afraid to trust."

He held his breath as several seconds ticked by.

There was a high probability she'd shut down, despite the door she'd cracked tonight with that kiss. Any second, she could stand and tell him to take a hike. Her hurt and fears ran deep, and he was venturing into restricted territory.

But as Jack had intuited, he was falling for this woman. Hard. And if she didn't trust him with her story, how could he ever win her heart?

Outside, a car passed, the blaring music seeping through the closed windows. A siren keened somewhere in the distance. The drip of a faucet tapped out a steady, monotone rhythm.

Just when he'd given up on the hoped-for breakthrough, Laura spoke in a small, quiet voice. "I've never shared my story with anyone."

He studied her. "Not even Sam?"

"No. She knows some of it, because she was involved the night this happened." Laura brushed her fingers over her sundress in the region of the scar. "But I never wanted to talk about it. And I wouldn't even know where to start."

"Do you *want* to start? With me?" He held his breath.

"I can try."

Thank you, God!

"Why don't you tell me how you and Joe got together?"

She picked up a throw pillow. Hugged it against her ribs. "We were always together, for as far back as I can remember. We were a pair from the time we were children. I never dated anyone else. When I was eighteen and he was twenty, we decided to get married, even though my parents weren't too excited about that."

That piece he knew, thanks to his late-night conversation with her mother during their Fourth of July visit.

"How did you end up in St. Louis?"

"Joe had an associate's degree in data processing, which made him well educated in our hometown, and he had big dreams. So we moved here, with not much more than hope to sustain us. But he couldn't compete with people who had four-year degrees and MBAs. He finally got a low-paying job as a data entry clerk, and I worked in a department store to help make ends meet."

When she paused, Nick gave her fingers an encouraging squeeze. He'd feed her questions if she faltered, but otherwise it would be best to let her tell her story at the pace and in the order she chose.

After a few moments, she continued "As time went on, Joe began to lose heart. It was clear that his only hope of advancing was to get more education, but he had no interest in going back to school. I realized then that if we were ever going to have a better life, it was up to me to take the initiative. So *I* went back to school. Since I'd worked every summer in a greenhouse at home, I got a job at a nursery and began to take classes in landscape design. When I discovered I had a knack for it, I decided to go on for my degree."

That sounded like the strong, take-charge woman he was coming to love.

"I can't pinpoint the moment when everything took a turn for the worse." Laura's voice was quieter and less steady now. "It happened gradually. Joe was frustrated, and he resented my ambition. He started to drink, and a side of him emerged that I'd never seen before. He'd get belligerent when he was drunk, and push me around. He began to belittle my efforts to get an education. Then he started making fun of my appearance, especially my weight, which was dropping. He said that if I'd been more supportive he would never have resorted to alcohol. He…he even laughed at my faith."

As her voice choked, Nick eased closer. Stroked a finger down her cheek.

How could anyone hurt this caring, compassionate woman who deserved only kindness?

"J-Joe began to lose jobs, one after another, until finally he quit working. Our life grew more and more isolated. If I hadn't had school and Sam and my church, I doubt I would have been able to cope. Those were the only normal things in my life—and my family, of course, even though I never told them any of this. What was the point of upsetting them because of a mistake I'd made?" Her voice choked, and she dipped her chin.

Typical Laura. Always thinking about others more than herself.

He stroked her hair, but when the silence lengthened he threw in a question that might help take the edge off her pain for a moment, give her a chance to collect herself. "How did you and Sam connect? You two seem very…different." A gross understatement. Girl next door and single swinger were opposite ends of the spectrum.

The corners of Laura's lips rose a hair. "Mutt and Jeff, as Sam likes to call us. I met her in the ladies' room when we were both going to night school. We ran into each other a few more times, and something clicked. We've been best friends ever since. That's why I called her the night…the night I left Joe. The night this happened." She touched the scar again.

"Tell me about that night."

She clenched her fingers around the edge of the pillow. "I'd been trying for months to convince Joe to get help, but whenever I brought it up he got angry. The incident that produced the scar happened the last time I suggested it. Believe it or not, it was our fourth anniversary." A tear brimmed on her lower lashes. Trailed down her cheek.

Gut clenching, he reached over and gently swiped it away.

"Sorry." She sniffed. "I thought I'd used up all my t-tears."

"No apology necessary. Do you want to take a break?"

"No. If I stop, I may never start again." She drew a ragged breath, and when she continued her words were choppy. "It was late. I was asleep. A crash from the living room woke me up, and I ran in to see what had happened. There was a broken whiskey bottle on the floor, and I went over to help Joe clean it up. But he…he slapped me, and he started saying…terrible things. I got scared and backed away. When I pleaded with him again to get help, he got more angry. The next thing I knew, he picked up the broken bottle and threw it at me. It hit me here." She touched the scar again.

Nick's rage swelled, and he fisted the fingers of his free hand. Took a steadying breath. "What happened next?"

"At first, I didn't know what to do. It was the middle of the night. But Joe was more violent than I'd ever seen him. So in the end, I threw on a jacket, grabbed my purse and phone, and walked to a twenty-four-hour quick shop that was nearby. Then I called Sam."

"And she came?"

"Within twenty minutes."

God bless her.

"Did you get medical attention?"

"Yes. I didn't want to, but Sam convinced me to go to the ER. Of course they asked questions, and even though I was vague about what happened they called the police." She hugged the pillow tighter. "Sam tried to get me to press charges, but I couldn't do that. Joe's life was already falling apart, and that would have demolished it. But I did decide to leave him. Sam played sentry the next day when I want back to the apartment to collect my things while he was out, and she insisted I stay with her until I found my own place."

"Did he try to convince you to come back?"

"Yes. But Sam told him to keep his distance or she'd call the police. She can be pretty assertive, in case you haven't picked that up."

"I noticed." Though he might have chosen a stronger word, like brash or forceful. Didn't matter, though. He was just grateful Laura had had a loyal friend by her side through all that trauma. "Did you ever consider going back?"

"Yes. I believed in the vows I took, including 'for better or worse.' Divorce was anathema to me. But my minister advised me to put my personal safety first, and Sam was very vocal in her opinion on the matter. Plus, the love I'd once felt for Joe had died. All that was left was fear. Still, I felt guilty about leaving him. I kept wondering if there wasn't more I could have done to convince him to get help."

"It sounds to me like you did everything you could. And if you'd stayed, you could have ended up dead."

"That's what Sam said." She shifted on the couch, wincing. "In the end, all my angst came to naught anyway. Joe was killed in a car accident two months after I left him."

"And you started over." A monumental task, in light of all she'd been through. One that would have felled a person with less grit and fortitude than the woman sitting beside him, whose deceptively fragile appearance masked a spine of steel.

"Yes. I got an apartment, applied for an educational grant, went to school full time, and worked a forty-hour week. Eighteen-hour days were the norm. Money was tight, and I lived on peanut butter sandwiches and macaroni and cheese for years. But I made it. I finished school and I got a job with a landscaper."

"How did you end up with your own company?"

"I had Joe's life insurance payout in reserve, which gave me the seed money to start my business after I'd accumulated a little experience. That was six years ago, and I've poured every cent back into the business since then. Thanks to the arts center job, I've turned the corner." She released a shuddering breath. "And now you know everything."

Not quite.

But he could surmise the rest, including the emotional toll her life with Joe had exacted. The years of living in constant fear. Her crushing guilt and disillusionment. The pain of betrayal that had made her terrified to trust again. The lost illusions of youth.

A constant economic grind that never rose above a hardscrabble existence. All the lonely years with no hand to hold and no one to share her life with. The choking self-doubt that prevented her from giving love another chance.

What a terrible legacy to have from a marriage.

Throat constricting, he slipped his arm around her shoulders and pressed the uninjured side of her face to his chest as another tear tracked down her cheek. "It's okay to cry."

"I don't c-cry."

"Maybe you should. Maybe you deserve to." He spoke the words against her hair, then grazed his lips across her forehead.

"It will h-hurt too much." She hiccupped the words as she pressed the pillow against her ribs.

That was probably true.

So he just held her until her trembling subsided and her breathing evened out.

At last she drew back far enough to search his eyes. "After the story I just told you, I wouldn't blame you if you decided to cut your losses and run."

He shook his head. "I don't plan to go anywhere—unless you tell me to take a hike."

"That's not in my plans." She moistened her lips. "But I'm still nervous about getting into a relationship. Being so wrong about someone you've known all your life can undermine your confidence in your judgment."

"Not everyone reacts well to adversity and disappointment, Laura. You had no way of knowing what would happen when Joe was put to the test."

She dipped her chin. "I guess not." But she didn't sound convinced.

"Hey." He waited until she looked at him. "All I'm asking

for is a chance to prove that with me, what you see is what you get. And I'll hang in as long as that takes. Fair enough?"

"More fair to me than to you, I think. I doubt most of the women you date drag their feet."

On the contrary, but he left that unsaid.

"Dated. Past tense. Going forward, I'm exclusive to you."

Her lips flexed into a wry twist. "No pressure there."

"None intended. I just want to make my intentions crystal-clear. But I do expect a few perks in return. Like the one you gave me when I got here."

A faint hint of pink mitigated some of her pallor. "I think that could be arranged." A yawn sneaked up on her, and she clapped a hand over her mouth. "Sorry. It's not the company."

His cue to exit.

But that was okay. They'd made tremendous progress tonight.

He stood. "You need to rest."

"I have to admit I'm starting to wilt." She pushed herself to her feet. "I'll walk you to the door."

He followed as she led the way, her usual full-speed-ahead stride a shadow of its former self as she shuffled across the room, one hand pressed against her ribs.

When she opened the door, she kept a firm grip on the edge, as if she needed the support to keep herself upright.

"Are you sure you'll be okay here by yourself tonight? I can stay if you want me to." He frowned as he scrutinized her.

"No. Sleep in your own bed. But I appreciate the offer, and also the dinner you brought."

"And I appreciate you trusting me with your story." He trailed his fingers gently down the uninjured side of her face. Then he stepped closer, slid his hand beneath her hair, and cupped the back of her neck with his palm. "Could we say good-bye the same way we said hello?"

"I hope so."

He leaned down to claim her lips, taking care not to press against her nose. When he finally drew back a couple of inches, her breath was warm on his cheek. "For the record, I can do a much better job of this. Which I'll demonstrate when your face isn't a minefield of bruises."

"Is that a…a promise?"

Her flirty comeback sent a zing through him. "Count on it. In the meantime, pencil me in for tomorrow night. Pizza okay for dinner?"

"You don't have to feed me again."

"If you don't share my pizza, I'll be eating alone."

Her mouth curved up. "Do you always get what you want?"

He reached over and fingered her hair. "That remains to be seen." After a moment, he stepped back. "If you need anything—day or night—call me."

"Thank you, but I'll be fine. Like I've told you before, I'm used to taking care of myself."

While that was true, if everything worked out as he hoped she wouldn't have to be a one-woman show going forward.

But he kept that to himself too. Those kinds of remarks at this stage could backfire.

With one last squeeze of her fingers, he turned and made his way down the stairs, a new spring in his step.

Tonight they'd entered new territory. Laura had not only opened her heart, she'd invited him in.

And barring some sort of major setback, it should be smoother sailing from here on out.

13

Life was sweet.

Smiling, Laura stretched awake, finally free of the lingering effects of the mugging. It had taken almost three months for the nagging pain in her ribs to subside, and finding a comfortable sleeping position had been a challenge for weeks, but at last she'd healed.

And not just physically.

Thanks to Nick, her battered heart and tattered trust were also mending. He'd become her wake-up call each morning, and on the rare evenings they didn't spend together, his was her last call of the day, the deep timbre of his voice lingering in her mind long after the connection had been severed.

In between, he pulled her away for impromptu picnics, dropped by to take her to Ted Drewes, or texted her funny memes. In fact, he'd become such an integral part of her world that it was getting hard to remember her life before him.

Still smiling, she swung her feet to the floor and stood, shifting gears as she mentally ran through her agenda for the day. Visits to the current job sites, of course, followed by a meeting with a potential new client who owned an upscale condo development in need of a major landscaping makeover.

If this kept up, she'd have to increase her staff yet again. No complaints, though. Business was good.

As was life.

And her new optimism was showing, according to Sam, who'd commented not long ago on her glow.

She walked toward her closet, but when her phone began to vibrate on the nightstand she pivoted and retraced her steps as. No doubt it was Nick, making his usual morning call.

But when she picked up her cell, the name of the accountant she'd hired after the arts center project prompted a huge growth spurt flashed on the screen.

Odd.

After their initial meeting, they rarely talked by phone. An occasional text sufficed. He was adept at his job, and the bookkeeping, payroll, and billing system he'd set up had been running like clockwork.

She pressed talk and put the phone to her ear. "Hi, Phil. What's up?"

"Sorry to bother you early in the morning, Laura, but I know once your day gets rolling it can be hard to catch up with you. I wanted to alert you to a potential issue with a couple of outstanding bills."

"How overdue are they?" And why call her about this? They had a process in place to handle delinquent accounts.

"One is from three months ago. The other is from last month."

"Have we sent the usual overdue notices?"

"Yes. That's where this gets tricky. After they got the notices, both clients called to tell me they'd paid their bill by check."

Frowning, she propped her hand on her hip. "Could the checks have been lost in the mail?"

"I asked. Both clients said they personally handed a check

for the full amount to your foreman. And both checks were cashed."

What?

A tiny chill rippled through her. "How much are we talking about between the two checks?"

"More than ten thousand dollars."

Her heart skipped a beat.

For an operation her size, which still operated on razor-thin margins despite the recent surge in work, that kind of loss would be a huge hit.

"Okay." She took a deep breath, trying to remain calm. "Maybe there's an explanation for this. Let me talk to Ken."

"Sorry to be the bearer of bad news."

"Not your fault. And I appreciate your diligence. Will you email me a copy of the two invoices?"

"As soon as we hang up."

"Thanks. I'll be back in touch ASAP."

She ended the call. Massaged her temples.

This wasn't making sense.

She'd vetted Ken thoroughly before hiring him. Done all the usual due diligence, including checking his references, experience, and credit rating. He'd not only been personable, he'd been clean as a whistle. And he'd done excellent work for her since being hired.

What on earth was going on?

But speculating wasn't going to give her answers. The two of them needed to have a face-to-face. In her office, not on a job site.

She lifted her phone again and set her fingers to work composing a text to him.

Need to talk to you. Can you swing by the office at nine?

Half a minute later, her phone pinged.

Sure. Something come up?

She hesitated for a moment, then typed in a response.

Need to discuss a couple of jobs. See you then.

Next, she typed a text to Nick to head off his usual morning call.

Issue came up at work. On the run this a.m. Talk to you soon.

Okay. I'll touch base later.

Laura moved into high gear, condensing her usual morning routine and bypassing breakfast. The roiling in her stomach was making her queasy, anyway.

But she did place a quick call to her attorney to get his input in case this situation was as bad as it sounded.

Unfortunately, that conversation wasn't comforting.

According to him, the time, money, energy, and legal fees involved in filing reports and pressing charges would in all likelihood exceed the cost of the loss. And after doing all that, the odds of recouping the stolen money were small.

Which left her few options other than asking Ken to repay

the funds—assuming he'd taken them—or eating the loss if he refused.

By eight-fifty, she was at her desk in the office adjacent to the equipment shed, copies of the two invoices in a folder in front of her. Five minutes later, Ken's car rolled through the gate of the small fenced compound that housed her supplies, equipment, and office.

Her pulse accelerated as she watched through the window while he approached.

Confrontation was always unpleasant. And after her experience with Joe, she'd come to hate it with a passion.

But there was no way around it today.

Ken parked near her door, slid from behind the wheel, and raised a hand in greeting to her through the window. After a quick knock, he stuck his head in and smiled. "You ready for me?"

No, she wasn't.

Yet what choice did she have?

"Yes. Come in." She motioned to the chair across from her desk.

He sat and crossed an ankle over a knee, his manner as engaging and straightforward as always. "This must be important if you pulled me off a job site."

Maybe, just maybe, this was all a misunderstanding. Perhaps he'd lost the checks, forgotten about them, and someone else had found them and cashed them.

But more likely she was grasping at straws because she didn't want to believe the obvious conclusion.

"It is." She filled her lungs. Slid the file across the desk toward him. "I wanted to talk about these."

He cocked his head as he regarded her, then leaned forward and picked up the folder. Flipped it open. Scanned the two sheets.

A muscle in his jaw ticced, and her stomach bottomed out.

She hadn't misread the situation. He knew exactly what this was about.

Because he'd taken the checks.

But she waited for him to speak.

"What would you like to know?" His tone was cautious when he looked at her, as if he was trying to decide how much she knew.

"I'd like to know what happened to the checks those clients gave you to pay their bills. I spoke with my accountant this morning, and both clients told him they handed you their checks—and the checks were cashed."

Ken closed the file. Set it back on the desk. "I'm going to be honest, okay? I like to gamble. I've always been able to control it, but not as much over the past year. I used those checks to pay off debts. I'd hoped to settle the two bills with money orders before the missing checks were discovered, but I never had the funds. I'm sorry."

Laura stared at him.

He hadn't tried to deny his culpability. On the contrary. His frank admission sounded almost perfunctory.

As for his apology, was he sorry he'd stolen, or sorry he'd gotten caught before he could fix the problem?

Didn't matter.

The deed was done, and the trust between them was shattered.

She folded her hands on her desk. "I'm sorry too. You're a good worker. I thought the two of us would have a long professional relationship. But I can't have people on my staff who aren't trustworthy. Your employment with me is ended as of now. Do you still intend to repay what you stole?"

"I don't have the funds to do that."

"We could work out a repayment plan."

He rested his elbows on the arms of his chair and linked his fingers. "I can't promise I could live up to it. I'm in debt again."

So he'd learned nothing from his experience.

"It sounds to me like you have a gambling addiction."

"Liking to gamble isn't the same as an addiction. I've just had a run of bad luck. So are you going to press charges? Because it's probably not worth the expense involved."

He'd done his homework, maybe in anticipation of this very day.

"I don't know yet. Probably not, if you pay me back."

"I don't know how long that would take."

"A good-faith effort would make me less inclined to pursue this."

He scrutinized her for a moment, then stood. "Let me think about it."

In other words, he was calling her bluff about the threat of a lawsuit. Once he walked out the door, she was never going to hear from him again unless she took legal action.

Which she couldn't afford to do.

Stomach churning, she rose too. "I need your key to this compound and the truck."

In silence, he pulled them out of his pocket. Laid them on the desk. "Thanks for the job. I'm sorry it didn't work out." Then he turned on his heel and exited.

She watched through the window as he slid behind the wheel of his car and drove through the gate.

Only then did she sink back into her desk chair and bury her face in her hands.

How could she have been so wrong about someone *again*? Just like Joe, Ken had presented one image to the world but had turned out to have an unsavory side.

And how was she supposed to cope at work without a foreman?

Bottom line, she couldn't. Meaning she'd have to take on that role again, along with her design work, until she hired someone new for that job. Which could take a while, because this go-round she was going to take extra time finding and vetting candidates. Even then, she'd keep close tabs on whoever she hired until she was absolutely certain they were trustworthy.

But until that happened, she was back to long hours and major belt-tightening.

Because the corner she thought she'd turned in her business had just become a dead end.

* * *

This could be a mistake.

But he'd run out of options.

Nick checked his watch and paced in front of the house in Webster Groves where he'd asked Laura to meet him.

For the past month, ever since her foreman's betrayal, she'd been working herself into the ground, putting in a ridiculous number of hours. The few times she'd managed to eke out a couple of hours for a date, she'd been exhausted and distracted.

Even worse?

All the groundwork he'd laid with her—all the small, undemanding physical intimacies he'd woven into their relationship over the past few months to demonstrate his trustworthiness and patience—was crumbling. The tentative touches she'd begun to initiate, which did more for his libido than any of the amorous ploys of the more sophisticated women of his acquaintance, had dried up.

Day by day, she was slipping away from him. Rebuilding the walls he'd begun to breach.

That's why it was time for desperate measures.

Except now he was having second thoughts.

Because this might be his only shot at the gold ring, and if she backed off, where did that leave him?

Before he could wrestle again with the question that had been keeping him awake at night, Laura pulled up in front of the house and parked under one of the colorful maples that lined the street on this late October day.

This was it.

Tamping down his worst case of nerves since he'd sat for the Architect Registration Exam, he shoved his fingers into the back pockets of his jeans and waited as she slid from behind the wheel and joined him.

She flashed him a quick smile and gave the old frame Victorian a scan. "Nice house."

No surprise that she liked it. It was the kind of house she'd once described as her dream home. Set far back from the street, on about an acre of ground, it was everything a Victorian should be, with gingerbread accents and a wraparound porch.

"And it's got great bones."

"I take it the new owner wants to make some changes?" She nodded toward the For Sale sign on the lawn.

"A few. I've already been inside, so we can skip that and go around to the backyard. Unless, of course, you'd like to take a look?" He dangled the key in front of her.

"Can I?" Her eyes lit up. "I've been itching to get inside one of these houses ever since I moved to St. Louis."

"I figured that might be the case. Follow me." He ascended the steps to the porch, fitted the key in the lock, and pushed the door open. "After you."

He followed her in, tagging along as she effused over all the things he'd had a feeling she'd love—the tall ceilings, gleaming hardwood floors, private nooks and crannies and alcoves, multiple fireplaces, the L-shaped stairway in the foyer that hugged the wall, art glass windows, wood moldings, and marble mantels.

When she'd explored every inch, she turned to him, her face more alive than it had been in weeks. "I don't know what the new owners have in mind, but I wouldn't change a thing. It's perfect."

"If all my clients were that satisfied with the status quo, I'd be out of business."

"You aren't going to do anything to change the character, are you?"

"No. Just some minor updating. Ready to take a look at the grounds?"

"Sure." But she seemed in no hurry to leave as she gave the foyer one more sweep. "Can you imagine this house at Christmastime, with snow on the ground, golden light shining from the windows, smoke curling above the chimneys, a wreath on the door? It's a perfect old-fashioned Christmas house. So warm and welcoming." She sighed. "What a wonderful place to call home."

"I couldn't agree more. Let me show you the backyard."

After they circled the house, he waited while she inspected

the grounds from all angles. In many ways it was a blank canvas. The yard was heavily shrubbed on the edges, affording complete privacy, and several big trees were spaced over the lawn, but little had been done in the way of landscaping.

At last Laura rejoined him. "My first thought is a gazebo—white lattice, of course. And a formal rose garden is a must. I also see a trellis overflowing with morning glories that leads to a private area with a bench and a birdbath and an English woodland garden. But there should also be plenty of open space for croquet games. This is a perfect yard for that." She turned to him. "Is the client open to suggestions, or do they have preconceived ideas?"

The moment had come.

Pulse galloping, he motioned toward a stone bench set beneath a maple tree adorned with brilliant red leaves. "Let's sit for a minute."

She squinted at him. "What's wrong?"

"Nothing, I hope. Come on, sit with me." He took her hand and led her to the bench. Once they were side-by-side, he swallowed. "You asked about the client. As a matter of fact, I know him well. Because potentially, it's me. I put an option on this house."

Her face went blank. "What?"

"I'm thinking of buying this house…but only if you'd like to share it with me." Slowly he withdrew the ring box from his pocket. "I realize we've only known each other six months. And I'm fine with a long engagement. But I know as surely as I know the sun will rise tomorrow that we belong together."

"Nick, I—"

"Wait." He held up a hand. "Please let me finish. I know this past month has been tough for you, and more than ever I want to be there for you every day, not just when you can fit me into your schedule. That's what love means. And I love you with all my heart. I can see us in this house, raising a family here, growing old together, sitting on the porch as our grandchildren play in the yard. I'm hoping you can see that too."

Several silent seconds passed, and then a single tear brimmed on her lower lashes. Trailed down her cheek.

It didn't look like a happy tear.

His stomach clenched, and he braced.

"I…I don't know what to say."

He forced up the corners of his mouth. "A yes would be great."

After a moment she eased her hand free. "It's not that I don't care for you, but marriage is a huge step. And I made a mistake once before."

"That was a long time ago. You were only eighteen—just a kid. And you had no way of knowing what would happen with Joe."

Her face was a study in misery as she looked at him. "But maybe I should have. I'd known him my whole life, and I still made a bad judgment call. I didn't see what was below the surface. Then I did it again as an adult, with Ken." Her shoulders slumped. "I have no confidence in my judgment skills, Nick. And I can't go through what happened with Joe again."

Hurt ricocheted through him. "I'm not Joe, Laura. Over the past few months I've done everything I can to prove to you that I'm trustworthy and dependable and even-tempered—and that I love you and respect you and would do everything in my power to protect you and care for you and be there for you."

"I know." The shattered look in her eyes gnawed at his gut. "The failure is mine, not yours. I told you at the beginning I was a long shot, and this proves it. If someone like you can't help me get over my fears, I doubt I'll ever overcome them." Her voice broke, and she swiped at her eyes. "I'm sorry, Nick. You deserve someone better than m-me."

As a vise slowly squeezed the life from his heart, he looked again at the house he'd hoped to share with the woman he loved. "There'll never be anyone better for me. And I'm sorry too." He slid the ring box back into his pocket, his fingers as shaky as the time he'd had the worst case of flu in his life. And he felt just as sick now. Then he stood.

She rose too, the flare of desperation in her eyes hollowing out his stomach. "Is this it?"

"I can't see a path forward, Laura. I'm patient, but I'm not getting the feeling my patience will ever be rewarded."

She didn't try to reassure him. "I-I'll miss you."

"Likewise." He took her icy hands and leaned down. Brushed his lips over hers one last time. "I hope someday you meet someone you love enough to trust with your heart."

Then gritting his teeth, he forced himself to walk away.

Because what other choice was there?

He'd done everything he could to overcome Laura's doubts, to show her how much he cared, and it hadn't been enough.

And holding out hope for a happier outcome would only stretch this out longer and hurt him even more in the end.

As he turned the corner of the house, he glanced back.

Laura was sitting on the bench again, elbows on knees, her face in her hands, shoulders heaving.

The woman who never cried was weeping, her sobs silent in the still air.

The world misted, and he swiped a hand across his eyes as the sun darted behind a cloud, turning the air as cold as his heart.

And as far as he could see, there was nothing he could do to warm it up.

14

Christmas was right around the corner, and Laura had never been in a less merry mood.

Sighing, she rooted through her frozen dinners and pulled out a chicken entrée. Extracted it from its box, vented the plastic covering, and stuck it in the microwave.

The only bright spot in her holiday season was that she'd finally found someone to replace Ken, which had allowed her to reduce her work schedule from an insane fourteen hours a day to a more manageable ten. And if her new foreman continued to prove he was reliable, she'd get back to eight or nine after the first of the year.

Not that she'd minded being busy these past two months, though. It gave her less time to think about Nick. Less time to be lonely. Less time to wonder if she'd made the biggest mistake of her life.

A very real possibility, even if she still couldn't corral her fears.

She crossed to the sink and filled a glass with water.

Besides, even if she wanted a second chance with him, why on earth would Nick give it to her? What guy would, after you'd thrown his proposal in his face, stomped on his heart, and told him you didn't trust him after all the months he'd spent proving he was an honorable man with impeccable integrity? After you'd snubbed his gentle understanding and tender kisses and infinite patience?

No man with a lick of pride would set himself up for another kick in the ego.

She kneaded the bridge of her nose.

She needed to get on with her life. Let him go. Pretend her heart wasn't broken.

And maybe, in time, she'd come to believe that lie.

The microwave pinged, and as she started back toward it the doorbell rang.

Huh.

Few people made their way up to her second-story apartment uninvited, and there was no one on her guest list tonight. Or any night, for that matter.

Wiping her palms on her leggings, she crossed to the door and peeked through the peephole.

Sam was here?

This would be the bright spot in her day.

Lips bowing, she pulled open the door. "What a nice surprise."

"And I come bearing gifts." Sam lifted a package wrapped in festive paper and sauntered in. "I can't stay. I'm on my way to an open house in the city, but since I was in the neighborhood I decided to drop off my Christmas gift. I'm not sure I'll see you again before I leave for Chicago for the holiday."

"I was going to stop by your place with your gift in a couple of days, so this saves me a trip. Would you like something to drink?"

"No, thanks. Libations will be flowing freely at the party I'm attending." She continued into the living room and sat on the couch.

"Let me grab your present." Laura detoured to her bedroom and retrieved Sam's package from her closet. Held it out when she returned. "Merry Christmas."

"Pretty." Sam fingered the holly sprig tucked into the bow. "Who goes first?"

"You." Laura sat beside her.

Sam tore the paper off the gift, lifted the lid, and pulled the two items from the box. "Ooh. Bubbles for my bath. And a scented candle. I see some luxurious soaks in my future."

"There's more in there."

Sam dug back in and withdrew an envelope. Pulled out the sheet inside. "Oh! A manicure at my favorite salon." Forehead scrunching, she shook her head. "This is too much, Laura."

"Never. I'm forever in your debt after all you've done for me."

"Nope. Friends have no debts between them. And I know money is tight for you right now. The bubble bath and candle would have been more than enough."

"Too late. I already threw away the receipts. Just enjoy the gifts." She leaned over and gave her a hug.

"Count on it." Sam squeezed her back then waved toward the package she'd brought. "Now open mine."

Laura picked it up and carefully peeled back the paper from the flat box. Opened the lid and scanned the gift certificate for a pedicure and a facial at a local day spa. "Speaking of too much…"

"You deserve a little indulgence."

"I've never had a professional pedicure. Or a facial."

"It's time you did." Sam reached over and squeezed her hand. "When are you going home for Christmas?"

She averted her face and set the box and certificate beside

her on the couch. "I'm not. I'm staying in town this year."

When Sam didn't respond, she peeked over to find her friend frowning at her. "Why?

"Mom decided to visit her brother and his family in California."

"What about *your* brothers?"

She shrugged. "John and Dana invited me and Dennis, but trying to be jolly in front of my family would take too much effort."

"Did you ever tell them what happened with Nick?"

"No. They never knew it was starting to get serious."

Sam crossed her legs. "Have you heard from him?"

"No. I didn't expect to."

"Are you having any second thoughts about dumping him?"

She winced at the harsh term. "I didn't dump exactly. I just…I just got scared."

"I get that. I mean, you've never shared the details with me about what happened with Joe, but I picked you up the night you left him, and I saw how sad you always were before that. It didn't take a math whiz to put two and two together. But you know what? Going through life afraid isn't really living. Remember what John Wayne said—courage is being scared to death but saddling up anyway. You need to saddle up, kiddo. And from what I've seen, Nick is worth saddling up for."

Laura twisted her hands together in her lap. "Even if I wanted to do that, it's too late. Why would he take me back at this point? It would be hugely hurtful to a guy for a woman to more or less tell him she doesn't trust him."

"So apologize."

"You make it sound easy."

"Maybe it is." Sam leaned toward her. "I'm no expert on

romance. I picked a loser the first time too. But I'm older and wiser—and so are you. We've got a new year staring us in the face. My advice to you is make a fresh start. Joe's been gone a long time, but he's still wrecking your life. Still running the show. You need to close the curtain on that act and move on."

Laura sighed. "Nick said almost the same thing. And I was on the verge of taking a leap. But after my bad judgment call about Ken, all my old fears resurfaced."

"You're being way too critical about your judgment. You picked me for a best friend, and look how great that turned out." Sam smirked and gave her an elbow nudge. "But seriously, you run a successful business, you supervise a large crew, and you deal with clients every day. So you ran into one bad apple in the business world. Join the club, kiddo. I've met more than my share of slimy characters in the workforce. Trust your heart. Trust Nick." She stood. "And with that bit of wisdom, I'll say good night."

Laura stood too and walked her to the door. "You're always a fount of practical advice. I'll think about what you said."

"Don't think too long. Guys like Nick don't come along every day." She leaned over and pulled her into a hug. "Merry Christmas. If I didn't have locked-in-stone plans for the holiday, I'd cancel and spend the day with you. I hate the thought of you being here by yourself."

"I'll be fine. And I won't be alone. I have church on Christmas Eve, and I'll talk to my family by phone on Christmas Day."

"And maybe Nick will be in your holiday mix, if you dig deep for courage and saddle up."

"I expect he went home to Denver for Christmas."

"Well, a girl can hope." With a grin and a thumbs-up, Sam disappeared down the steps.

Silence descended after she left, and Laura wandered back to the kitchen. Retrieved her cooling dinner. Sat at the table and poked at it with a fork.

This was nothing like the cozy meals she and Nick had shared over the past months at this table, filled with lively conversation and smiles and laughter.

The kind of dinners she could have looked forward to every night if she'd had the guts to put aside her fears and have faith in the man who'd tried so hard to earn her trust.

Setting her fork down, she closed her eyes. Folded her hands. And did what she'd been doing every day for months.

She prayed.

For guidance—and for the strength to follow wherever that direction might lead.

* * *

Christmas Eve had arrived.

But there was no joy in Laura's world.

After closing and locking up the office at three o'clock, she trudged to her truck.

What could she do to fill the four hours before the evening service at church?

Strolling around a mall amid the throng of merry, last-minute shoppers would be too depressing. And her apartment felt empty and hollow these days.

Best plan? Stop somewhere for a fast-food dinner, swing by her apartment to change, then continue on to church. It would be open early on Christmas Eve, and an hour or so of quiet time there before the service began might help her sort through her muddled thoughts.

She followed that plan to the letter, but unfortunately she still had no clear guidance by the time the church began filling with people for the candlelight service.

That changed, however, as Brad Matthews launched into his sermon.

In fact, the childhood friend who'd offered her a sympathetic ear and sound advice during her darkest days seemed to have written it just for her. Especially the conclusion.

"Tomorrow most of us will exchange gifts wrapped in festive paper with the ones we love. But those material gifts are only meant to represent the true gift of this season—the gift of love. And by sending us his son, God gave us a shining example of what love is at its very best. It's unselfish. Trusting. Enduring. Forgiving. Limitless. Unconditional.

"Of course, for humans that example can be difficult to emulate. Because love can be very hard. And it can break. But it can also be mended. Sometimes all it takes is two simple words, spoken from the heart: I'm sorry. So during this Christmas season, give yourself a gift. Mend a broken relationship and trust in the goodness of love."

For the rest of the service, those words resonated in Laura's mind as she sang the familiar hymns and recited the common prayers, mingling with the advice Sam had offered.

Don't go through life afraid, because that isn't really living.

Saddle up even if you're scared.

Apologize.

Close the curtain on the past and move on to the next act.

Mend a broken relationship.

Trust in the goodness of love.

And she could add one more piece of advice to that list, sourced from deep within.

Let yourself believe once again in happy endings.

A gentle snow was falling when she emerged from the church after the service, so at odds with the turmoil of her thoughts. And as she climbed into her truck, an image of the cozy Victorian house Nick had lovingly chosen for them flashed across her mind.

A pang echoed in her heart.

It was probably filled with laughter and music and love as the new owners enjoyed their first Christmas there.

A sudden yearning to see it swept over her, and since she had only an empty apartment to return to, she put the truck in gear and headed for the house that had come to represent Nick's love and the life he'd offered her.

When she reached the street, Laura drove slowly down the pavement that was beginning to disappear under the large flakes drifting down from the heavens.

As she approached the house, she frowned.

The windows were all dark, and the For Sale sign remained on the lawn.

How could a gem like this still be unsold?

The street was lined with cars, no doubt belonging to guests in the many houses that were festively lit for the season. But when she found a vacant spot farther up the block, she eased in and set the brake. Then, digging her hands into the pockets of her coat, she trudged up the sidewalk and stopped in front of the house.

It was every bit as beautiful as she remembered. But it was also empty and alone—just like she was.

Shoulders drooping, she scanned the empty street, then walked up the path to the front door, climbed the stairs, and sat on the top step. After folding her arms on her knees, she rested her forehead on her sleeves as an aching sense of regret flooded through her.

It was time to face the truth.

Love, in all its beauty, had been within her grasp and she'd let it slip away because she was afraid to take a chance on something that didn't come with guarantees or warranties.

Yet not every relationship crashed and burned.

So yes, she could go on playing it safe. Shunning risk. Locking her heart away behind an impenetrable wall.

But if she did, she'd spend the rest of her life alone instead of with the most wonderful man she'd ever met.

She choked back a sob.

Great as that insight was, it might have come too late. Despite Brad's assurance that broken relationships could be mended, she'd hurt Nick deeply with her lack of trust in him. Damaged their relationship, maybe beyond repair.

But in this season of hope, what could it hurt to reach out to him? Ask for forgiveness? Tell him how much she loved him?

And hope he gave her a second chance.

* * *

Was that Laura sitting on the steps of the old Victorian house he'd hoped to share with her?

Nick turned up the collar of his sheepskin-lined jacket and shoved his hands into the pockets as snowflakes drifted down around him, obscuring his view.

When she lifted her head, however, he had no problem identifying her.

But what was she doing here on Christmas Eve? Why hadn't she gone home for the holiday?

Was it possible she was as bummed about their break-up as he was, and like him had decided to forego the usual family festivities? Had she come here to think about what might have been, as he had?

And if so, could that possibly mean she might have regrets about their break-up? Maybe even be open to taking the step she'd backed away from in October?

Trying not to let himself get too carried away, he pushed through the gate and walked up the path, his footsteps silent on the snow-covered bricks.

A few feet from the porch he stopped. Gave up any attempt to rein in his galloping pulse as he took a gulp of cold air. "Hello, Laura."

Her head jerked up and she vaulted to her feet, eyes rounding. "Nick? Wh-what are you doing here?"

"You said once it would be beautiful at Christmastime, so I thought I'd take a look. I'm surprised it's still for sale."

"Me too."

A door opened nearby and the sound of carols and laughter drifted through the silent air.

"You didn't go home for Christmas?"

She shook her head. "I wasn't in the mood. But I thought you would."

"I wasn't in the mood either."

She bit her lip. Scuffed the toe of her boot in the snow. "I've missed you." Her voice was shaky, her gaze probing as she locked onto his face.

"I've missed you too."

"I've been thinking a lot about us these past couple of months."

"Me too." He bit back the questions that were clamoring for

release. It was best to let her say what she wanted to say without prompting.

And pray this was leading where he hoped it would.

"I owe you an apology."

His spirits sank.

Was that was this about? She was remorseful because she'd hurt him, not because she'd had a change of heart?

He fisted his hands in his pockets and tried to maintain a calm tone despite the sudden, sharp pain in the region of his heart. "Not necessary. I understand why you're afraid. I also know you're doing what you think you need to do to protect yourself from more hurt. You don't have to apologize for breaking up."

"But I want to apologize for way more than that. Although in hindsight that was a…a huge mistake."

She was sorry for the split?

His plummeting spirits reversed course. "I'm listening." Because he was *not* going to jump to any conclusions.

"Can we sit for a minute?" She motioned to the steps.

In silence he closed the distance between them and sank onto the tread beside her.

In spite of the dim light, it was easy to see that the past couple of months had taken a toll on her. There were shadows under her lower lashes, and faint lines at the corners of her eyes.

Maybe she'd been as lonely as he'd been.

She removed a pair of gloves from her pockets and tugged them on. "I don't really know where to start, except with I'm sorry. For so many things. For letting the past control my life. For being afraid to commit to you and not trusting you, when I've never met a more trustworthy person. For hurting you. For throwing away the beautiful gift you offered me." Her voice broke, and she angled toward him, irises shimmering. "These past two months have been so miserable and lonely without you. I want the same things you want, Nick—the rose garden and the picket fence and the family."

A blare of "Joy to the World" came through a door as it opened to admit more guests, and Laura sniffed. Swiped the back of her glove under her nose. "I realize I'm no bargain, and I know I still have issues to work through. But I'd like to work on them with you beside me. I know marriages don't come with lifetime warranties, but I promise to do my best to make you happy for as long as I live—if you can forgive me, and if the offer of that ring still stands."

As her words lingered in the quiet air, the knot that had been in his stomach for weeks began to loosen.

Except she still hadn't said the three words that mattered most.

"First of all, there's nothing to forgive. I'll admit I was hurt, but I understood why you were afraid. And I guess it was egotistical of me to think I could overcome years of debilitating fear in a few months. I probably should have waited on the proposal, but when you started to slip away I got desperate." A snowflake landed on her nose, and he reached over. Brushed it off. "But maybe it was providential. Because loneliness isn't enough of a reason to get married."

She stared at him. "Is that why you wanted to marry me?"

"No. I love you. I have for months."

Her forehead puckered. "I don't understand."

He reached over. Took her hand. "Laura. Why do you want to marry *me*?"

All at once light dawned in her eyes. "Did I forget to say I love you?"

He hiked up one side of his mouth. "I didn't hear those words."

"Oh, Nick. I've made such a colossal mess of this." She angled toward him and took his other hand. "Let me be absolutely clear. I love you with all my heart. I want to spend every day of the rest of my life with you. I want to wake up next to you in the morning and fall asleep in your arms. Fifty years from now, I want sit on this front porch with you and celebrate our golden wedding anniversary. Because you make the sun shine in my heart even on cloudy days. Good enough?"

Pressure built in his throat, and he stood. Pulled her up beside him. "Good enough. But love is about more than words, you know."

Her mouth curved up. "Are you saying you'd like a little action too?"

"I wouldn't object."

"In that case..." She erased the distance between them, put her arms around his neck, and lifted her face to him. "I'm all yours."

The sweetest words he'd ever heard.

And he wasted no time lowering his lips to hers, holding nothing back.

Neither did she.

And despite the frosty weather, he was as warm inside as—

"Excuse me…are you folks lost?"

He pulled back, but kept one arm around Laura as she turned toward the street.

An older man stood looking up at them from the sidewalk.

Nick smiled down at the woman he loved. "No. Not anymore. We just came home." Then he turned back toward the street. "We're going to buy this house."

The man beamed at them. "Now that's what I call a Christmas present."

Epilogue

"Welcome home, Mrs. Sinclair." Nick set the brake and turned off the engine in the driveway of the Victorian house where they were about to begin their life together.

At the tenderness in his eyes, pressure built in Laura's throat. "I like the sound of that."

"So do I. I'll get your door."

She waited as he circled the car, then took the hand he extended, pausing for a moment to look at the golden light spilling from the windows of their home. "It's beautiful, isn't it?"

"Beautiful is the perfect word."

But when she glanced at him, his gaze was on her, not the house.

"Compliments will get you everywhere."

"I hope so." He grinned and waggled his eyebrows. "But on a more serious note—are you sure you wouldn't have preferred the Ritz tonight?"

"This *is* my Ritz—as long as you're by my side." She smiled up at him.

"I have no intention of straying far." He took her hand, and together they walked to the front door.

Once he unlocked it, he pocketed his key—and before she realized his intent he swept her into his arms and lowered his lips to hers.

When the kiss intensified, Laura eased back. "Um…the neighbors could be watching."

"I suppose we should take this inside."

"Uh-huh."

After pushing through the door, he closed it with his foot and made a beeline for the staircase without ever putting her down.

She gave a soft laugh, even as a wave of excitement swept through her. "Anxious to get the honeymoon started, aren't we?"

"Guilty as charged."

When they reached the bedroom, he set her on her feet and removed the light wrap from around her shoulders. Soft, classical music played in the background, and the room was bathed in a gentle, subdued light.

Of course the man she loved would have set the scene for their arrival.

"I want to show you something" Nick took her hand and led her to the antique oval mirror on a stand in one corner of the room. He positioned her in front, then stood behind her and rested his hands on her shoulders. "What do you see?"

As she studied their reflections, joy and peace filled her.

Nick set her heart aflutter no matter what he wore, but in the tux that enhanced his striking good looks and broad shoulders he was every woman's dream groom.

And she looked like a glowing bride in her peach-colored tea-length lace gown, its sweetheart neckline and short, slightly gathered sleeves adding an old-fashioned charm. She'd also styled her hair the way Nick liked it, loose and full, the soft waves pulled back on one side with a small cluster of flowers and lacy ribbon.

But mostly what registered was the two of them, together, for life.

"Well?" Nick prompted.

"I see a miracle."

"I won't argue with that. But you know what else I see? The most beautiful bride that ever lived and the most wonderful, desirable woman I've ever met."

"Oh, Nick." Eyes misting, she turned and looped her arms around his neck. "I never thought I could be so happy."

His eyes softened. Warmed. "Get used to it, Mrs. Sinclair. Because happiness is exactly what I have planned for you for the next sixty or seventy years." He trailed his lips across her forehead, then eased away. "Don't go away. I'll be right back."

"I'll be waiting."

As Nick disappeared out the door, Laura gave the room they'd decorated together a slow scan.

They'd done well, choosing an English country style that suited the house. A canopy bed, two comfortable chairs by the fireplace, a crystal chandelier. And Nick had gone out of his way to make this night special. Two champagne glasses rested on a low table, and the subdued lighting and soft music created the perfect ambience for their first night together.

When Nick reentered, he nuzzled her neck. "Did you miss me?"

"As a matter of fact, I did." She leaned into his kiss.

"I brought some champagne." He held up the bottle.

"I saw the glasses."

"Will you have some?"

"Mm-hm."

He popped the cork, poured the bubbly liquid into the two waiting glasses, and bent to strike a match to the logs. They quickly flamed into life, sending shadows dancing on the walls, and Laura moved closer to the welcome warmth.

"Cold?" Nick asked as he handed her a glass.

"A little. It's on the chilly side for the first day of spring."

He gave her a slow smile. "I think we can take care of that. But first, a toast." He raised his glass. "To new beginnings—and a love that never ends"

Laura lifted her glass, and the bell-like tinkle as they clinked resonated in the room.

They both took several sips, and then Nick reached over and removed the glass from her fingers. Set the two glasses side by side on the mantel. Held out his hand.

And as she moved into his arms, Laura had one last coherent thought.

Second chances didn't get any better than this.

Keep reading for a preview of
A TIME TO LOVE,
Book 2 in the Circle of Friends series.

~Excerpt~

A Time to Love

CIRCLE OF FRIENDS—BOOK 2
ENCORE EDITION

1

"Well, kiddo, this is it." Samantha Reynolds closed the door of the bride's room after Laura Taylor's mother exited to take her walk down the aisle, then turned to face her best friend.

Laura's face was glowing. "I never thought this would happen. It feels almost too good to be true."

"I hear you. But trust me, it's true. And you deserve this happy ending." Sam gave Laura's peach-colored tea-length dress a sweep. So perfect for a second wedding, and for ultra-feminine Laura. As was her bouquet of ivory and peach roses intertwined with ivy and wispy fern. "You look gorgeous. Wait'll Nick gets an eyeful."

Laura reached for her purse and fished out a tissue. "I'm so happy it's almost scary."

"Hey! No tears. Your mascara will run and you'll look like a raccoon. Not a pretty picture, let me tell you." She grinned and gave Laura a shoulder nudge.

A knock sounded on the door, and Laura's brother stuck his head inside. "Ladies, it's your cue."

Sam gave Laura's hand a squeeze, then slipped out of the bride's room and took her place behind the double doors that led to the church. When the organ music paused, then changed melodies, two ushers pulled back the heavy doors.

She was on.

As Sam made her way past the sea of smiling faces, she took a deep breath of the fragrant rubrum lilies. Late-afternoon light illuminated the stained glass windows, which in turn cast a mosaic of warm, muted colors on the rich wood floor.

It was a beautiful and appropriate setting for Laura's wedding.

But the icing on the cake was her handsome, charming groom. Nick Sinclair was a patient, caring, decent man. In other words, exactly what Laura deserved.

She smiled and gave him a subtle thumbs-up as she took her place near the altar, and he grinned in return.

Once Laura entered, however, his attention remained riveted on her.

And at the tenderness and love in his eyes, Sam's throat constricted.

How amazing it must be to be loved like that.

And she couldn't be happier for her best friend.

Also a touch jealous.

Because much as she longed for her own happy ending, that wasn't in the cards.

Her vision misted, and she fumbled for the tissue she'd tucked into the tiny pocket of her pencil skirt. Tried to discreetly dab at her eyes.

But her subtle move caught the eye of the minister, a

childhood friend of Laura's.

He arched an eyebrow, as if to ask, *are you okay*?

Forcing up the corners of her lips, she nodded.

The ceremony continued, and when he launched into his remarks, she forced herself to focus on his mellow, soothing voice. Maybe that would keep the blues at bay until the ceremony was over.

While his praise for Laura and Nick was well deserved, what he said at the end resonated deeply.

The road of life *wasn't* always easy or straight. People made wrong turns, took detours, hit roadblocks, had flat tires. But according to him, if you kept your focus on the ultimate destination, you'd always find your way home.

It was a beautiful talk, filled with hope and promise—two things that had long been lacking in her life.

And it was a far cry from the fire and brimstone sermons of her youth.

As Laura and Nick prepared to exchange their vows, she dug out Nick's ring from her other pocket and moved closer to the couple.

But her focus wasn't on them. It was on the minister. Brad Matthews.

The man radiated character and kindness and integrity. And he was handsome. Late thirties or early forties, with silver-touched sandy brown hair and a toned physique. He also wore a wedding ring. Naturally.

Not that a man like him would ever have a remote interest in someone like her, anyway.

Especially a man of the cloth.

Quashing that depressing thought, she shifted her attention to the radiant bride for the remainder of the ceremony. Smiled for the staged wedding pictures. Gave an entertaining toast at the reception. Danced with the best man.

But once all the rituals were over, her spirits flagged again.

What she needed to do was find a quiet spot for a moment and try to stem the tsunami of emotions threatening to swamp her.

She eyed the door to the terrace.

It might be cool out there on this first day of spring, but enduring a slight chill was better than watching Laura and Nick gaze into each other's eyes as they danced to the romantic strains of "Our Love Is Here to Stay."

Because if she hung around, the wisecracking Sam the world knew just might break down in tears.

* * *

He didn't have the terrace to himself, after all.

Heaving a sigh, Brad Matthews hesitated as he stepped outside.

So much for a break from the festive celebration that reminded him too much of his own wedding day twelve years ago. The very reason why he rarely attended the receptions for marriages at which he officiated. It wasn't that he begrudged brides and grooms their happy ending. It was just too hard to be reminded time and again that the "after" in his own happily-ever had been short-lived.

Nor was he up to exchanging pleasantries with yet another wedding guest out here in the chilly evening air.

He started to turn away, but when the woman in the shadows at the edge of the terrace sniffed and angled sideways, he froze.

It was Sam Reynolds, the maid of honor.

It seemed the tears he'd detected in the sanctuary earlier were back.

Not what he'd expected, based on Laura's comments about her best friend through the years. Sam had sounded more like the upbeat, irreverent type who always had a firm grip on her emotions.

Maybe that's why she'd come out here. To hide an uncharacteristic display of weepiness. She probably wouldn't appreciate being caught in an emotional meltdown.

But when she sniffed again, and a choked sob broke the stillness, his ministerial instincts kicked in and words spilled out before he could stop them. "I don't mean to intrude, but is everything all right?"

Sam gasped and spun around, her hand flying to her chest. "Oh! You startled me."

"Sorry about that." He stayed where he was, giving her space to regroup.

A few beats ticked by, and when she spoke she sounded more in control. "No worries. I just didn't expect anyone else to brave the cold. It's pretty ch-chilly out here."

Especially in a short-sleeved lace jacket.

Without stopping to think, he slid his own jacket off, crossed to her, and draped it around her shoulders. "This may help."

"I shouldn't take your jacket. You'll get cold." Her objection was halfhearted at best as she drew it around herself.

"I'll be fine. It was getting warm in there." He tipped his head toward the banquet room.

In the silence, Brad studied her.

Laura often talked of Sam, and physically, he'd had her

pegged. Sophisticated makeup, svelte figure, striking sleek red hair. Shorter stature than he'd expected, though. He'd pictured her as statuesque to go with her larger-than-life, cheeky image. Instead, she was at least six inches shorter than his six-foot frame, even in her high heels.

But he'd been way off base on her demeanor and personality. Laura always talked about Sam's composure and self-confidence, described her as the strong, invincible type who was never thrown by anything and never at a loss for words.

Yet the woman who'd teared up during the ceremony and who now stood silent and subdued an arm's length away didn't fit that image at all.

"It was a beautiful wedding, wasn't it?" A bit inane, but it *was* the topic of the day. And safe, in case she thought he was being pushy.

"Yes. Very." She sniffed again, dabbing at her nose with a tissue as she gave him a shaky smile. "Sorry. I'm a sucker for happy endings."

Somehow that didn't ring true.

The Sam that Laura had described might be moved by her best friend's wedding, but she'd hide it behind a flippant remark. She wouldn't cry.

There was something else going on here.

About the Author

© DeWeesePhotography.com

Irene Hannon is the bestselling, award-winning author of more than sixty-five contemporary romance and romantic suspense novels. She is also a three-time winner of the RITA award—the "Oscar" of romance fiction—from Romance Writers of America, and a member of that organization's elite Hall of Fame.

Her many other awards include National Readers' Choice, Daphne du Maurier, Retailers' Choice, Booksellers' Best, Carol, and Reviewer's Choice from *RT Book Reviews* magazine, which also honored her with a Career Achievement award for her entire body of work. In addition, she is a HOLT medallion winner and a two-time Christy award finalist.

Millions of copies of her books have been sold worldwide, and her novels have been translated into multiple languages.

Irene, who holds a BA in psychology and an MA in journalism, juggled two careers for many years until she gave up her executive corporate communications position with a Fortune 500 company to write full-time. She is happy to say she has no regrets.

A trained vocalist, Irene has sung the leading role in numerous community musical theater productions and is a soloist at her church. She and her husband enjoy traveling, hiking, gardening, and spending time with family. They make their home in Missouri.

To learn more about Irene and her books, visit www.irenehannon.com. She loves to interact with readers on Facebook and is also active on Instagram.

Made in United States
Orlando, FL
11 April 2025

60394398R00125